Hartsfield-Jackson International Airport – the busiest airport in the world. More than 9,000 acres of concrete and steel dominating the south side of Atlanta. There are five runways crisscrossing the facility, made possible by more than 4.7 million cubic yards of ready-mix, enough to pave every street in Knoxville, Tennessee – twice. The impressive numbers don't stop there: 42 miles of escalator tread, 97 miles of moving sidewalks and enough rail to build a bullet train from Mobile, Alabama to somewhere in Mississippi

Every year, more than 100 million passengers have their patience tried by TSA agents, then weave their way through the maze of concourses to a gate and onto an aircraft, which comes in various shapes and sizes. The destinations are equally varied. It could be a domestic dash to Dayton, or a marathon trek to Tokyo.

The only certainties are:: 1) luggage will be lost in transit, and 2) someone will have failed their personal hygiene class in middle school and, in all likelihood, will be seated close to you.

Atlanta is the hub of the South. You don't lay claim to the title of busiest airport in the world without arrivals and departures clogging the air traffic control radar sunup to sundown and beyond. There is an old saying in the South. "When you die, you have to go through Atlanta to get to heaven."

There is another saying that is more in line with the pages that follow. "If you sit in the Atlanta airport long enough, you'll meet everyone you ever knew." One assumes that means those who are still alive. But if the shuttle from Kerr-Ransdall Funeral Home is making its way to heaven, you might just see someone you know among the ranks of the dearly departed.

We're not concerned with those we know — at least not in this space. We can recite their accomplishments and transgressions, some of which occur in close proximity to each other. For example, there is Rick Allen, a college friend who recently won the Volunteer of the Year Award from the local Chamber of Commerce.

Unfortunately, his extended celebration landed him in jail on a drunk and disorderly charge, and for soliciting a prostitute to liven up the festivities — a hooker named Dani Devine whose real name started with Detective. Local news coverage was quite interesting. There was a picture of him accepting the Chamber award on page 7; his mug shot from the arrest was on page 1.

We can explore what makes Rick tick anytime. Right now, we're more concerned with those we don't know; those we have managed to catch sight of in Concourse D of Hartsfield-Jackson.

Our focus is on flight 668 to Lexington, Kentucky, the mecca of Thoroughbred racing; Bluegrass and Bourbon; the bastion of old money and the Southern gentility one normally associates with it; the *haute veneer* that masks a seamier side of life that includes abject poverty, illiteracy, drugs and crime. Between those diametrically opposed extremes is a middle class propped up by the University of Kentucky and a healthcare facility on nearly every corner.

The traveling companions are an odd lot, not unlike the menagerie of folks in the Canterbury Tales. There is the personal injury lawyer in ill-fitting polyester suit studying briefs over a snifter of brandy. Actually, it's cheap Scotch in a wine glass thanks to his powers of persuasion with the bartender. To his left is a family of five: dad on his smart phone placing bets on the racing card at Aqueduct, which is anything but smart, mom in full panic mode as she reviews the family's check register, and stair-step daughters—8, 6, and 4—adorned in princess gowns and mouse ears.

These folks cannot be subject of our journey into their lives. One is too trite, the other too tragic. We can't focus on the college students returning from spring break, nor the drug store cowboy with more bullshit in his boots than on them. Not the retired couple returning from a visit to grandchildren they never see; not the businessman fighting to compete in a world that has changed despite his best efforts to keep things as they were in the 1980s; and it certainly can't be the tweens who have been to leadership camp where they all met their own Mr. Wonderful.

Then who?

Chapter 1 — Jack Adams

Jack was born for politics. His grandfather was so passionate about the sport that he insisted that his youngest daughter add Quincy as a moniker for newborn John Adams. It is, after all, Kentucky where your name means something, like the gentleman who legally changed his to tack on CPA in his run for state auditor. And then there was the treasurer candidate whose campaign material boldly proclaimed his name to be John Kennedy Hamilton.

We can't forget Ray "I'm a Democrat" Adkins. Nor can we ignore the Perkins family in Congress. Carl D. Perkins represented Kentucky's mountains for 35 years until his death in 1984. He was succeeded by his son, Christopher, who ran for his first congressional race as Carl C. Perkins even though he had been known as Chris his entire life. Most political observers at the time speculated that Appalachian folks thought they were voting for the old man.

Jack's pedigree may have had political bloodlines, but he developed an early fondness for football (and cheerleaders) more than public policy and political campaigns. All-state quarterback for his tiny team in Pike County; full ride athletic scholarship to the University of Louisville — the same institution that produced hall of famer, Johnny Unitas, and Heisman Trophy winner, Lamar Jackson. Jack was neither hall of fame nor Heisman material.

When it became abundantly clear that he wouldn't make the NFL draft, or even win a spot on an arena football team, he turned his attention to more important matters — partying, philandering, the occasional brush with the law, and frequent trips to the clinic for one more round of antibiotics.

After five years, he graduated. Granted it wasn't *magna cum laude*, or even *cum laude*, but it was a diploma he could call his own — only the second on his mother's side of the family, second only to his grandfather. It was the first earned by anyone on his father's side of the family, or at least that is what he was told because Dad didn't stick around too long after young Jack was born. Rumor had it that granddad had something to do with that as he did almost every aspect of Jack's life.

There he was. By the grace of God, and a generous check from his grandfather to the Alumni Association, Jack Adams was a college graduate with a degree in history. What one does with a history degree had never been a concern to him. Granddad would surely take care of him wherever future opportunities would lead.

His mother suggested teaching. That would bring him back home to Pike County where granddad could use his friendship with the school superintendent to land the new college grad a job as a teacher and a coach. Jack would have none of it. After five years of enjoying the night life River City had to offer, coal country had lost its luster. Besides, he already had bedded most of the attractive women in the county — both married and unmarried. He needed the bigger pool of candidates that Louisville had to offer.

His grandfather, his rock, his mentor, his confidant wanted Jack to go into the coal business with him. Long before Warren Buffet was credited with advising investors to buy when others are selling and sell when others are buying, Clement Combs masterered riding the frequent booms and busts of the coal industry. It allowed him to amass a small fortune — or perhaps, a fortune that was not so small.

He maintained the family homestead in Pikeville, but also had places to hang his hat in Louisville, Lexington, Savannah, the UP of Michigan, and Naples, Florida. Holdings beyond his coal operations included a community bank, a string of auto dealerships, a dozen or so fast food franchises, and — his personal favorite — an upscale motel in downtown Lexington. It afforded him an opportunity to further diversify his interests — blondes, brunettes *and* redheads — when Mrs. Combs accompanied him to town for University of Kentucky football and basketball games. She got the condo; he got what he called the condom suite.

Clement wanted to put Jack in charge of business development for his energy interests, which essentially would require him to wine and dine prospective partners in his grandfather's new ventures. The wining and dining sounded great, but Jack would have much preferred the company of the investors' wives and/or girlfriends. Yellow Creek Energy would have to look elsewhere for someone to schmooze in Clement's absence.

Two months after graduation, Jack was still wrestling with a career decision. Granddad Clement wasn't happy; his mother was despondent that he would not be returning home; Olivia, the on-again, off-again squeeze who had vowed to wait for him gave up in frustration and got pregnant by Jack's best friend.

Clement demanded that Jack choose something. He had been father and grandfather for the boy. More importantly from Jack's perspective, Clement had been his personal ATM. But the time had come to cut the cord. Clement's charge to Jack was to get into the family business, or get out on your own.

Then, Jack happened on a brilliant idea — extend his educational pursuits. Surely, Clement couldn't cut him off if he were working toward a graduate degree with the promise of a better equipped decision two or three years down the road. By then, Jack would be 25, mature enough to put down roots rather than sow wild oats. But what degree? Additional studies in history would make him a better educated but unemployable graduate. MBA sounded attractive, but his undergraduate studies didn't provide the prerequisites necessary and there was no way he would take on additional work at the undergrad level.

How about the law? Granddad could always keep an attorney on retainer; a very generous retainer. It would give him the cachet he needed to be recognized as one of the up-and-comers in polite Kentucky society, which of course meant a new cast of coquettes to conquer. As an attorney, he would have even more credibility in business development for his grandfather and all of the country club memberships, Keeneland boxes, Derby tickets, and mid field or mid court seats at UK and U of L that would follow.

That's it! That's the course he would take, the blueprint he would follow on his way to fame, fortune, and frequent trysts. He didn't know Archimedes from Archie Andrews, but he had no trouble quoting him, "Eureka, I have found it."

Only one obstacle stood in his way. The LSAT. He had difficulty with the written part of his driver's test; how the hell could he get a score on the LSAT that would get him into any law school, much less the Brandeis College of Law at U of L? As he pondered the dilemma over three fingers of Wild Turkey at his favorite Brownsboro Road bar, in walked Anthony Barrows who plopped his large frame on the adjacent barstool. Jack's life was about to change forever.

Chapter 2 — Big Tony

Anthony DeMarco Barrows was everything Jack Adams wasn't—in a bad way. Jack enjoyed the privilege of wealth, stature, and power. Big Tony, as he was called, was from the other side of those tracks where his family scraped by on the infrequent work his itinerant father could hold down, the meager wages his second-generation Italian mother earned as a housekeeper for a family whose patriarch's name was, oddly enough, Landon Gentry. And there were six children, which in itself was a miracle since his father was seldom home. He obviously mastered procreational efficiency.

All of the kids, four girls and two boys, did their share to earn money—mowing lawns, babysitting, raking leaves, tutoring younger children, and delivering newspapers.

The latter was the one where Anthony found his niche. It turned out, he was quite adept at making money from his two newspaper routes, and making friends among his customers, who eventually grew to admire the young man for his work ethic and wonder how Little Tony Barrows could be the father of someone so dedicated.

(As an aside, the names are correct. Anthony Dewayne Barrows—or Little Tony—was the father of six by Sophia Ricci. Their youngest son was named Anthony DeMarco Barrows to honor the father and maternal grandfather. The younger Anthony became Big Tony at age 12 when he surpassed his dad in both height and weight by some three inches and 20 pounds. It got more pronounced in the years that followed.)

There were two things Big Tony excelled at: creativity in making money and an uncanny ability to read and record in his gray matter all things relevant and all things trivial.

On the money-making side, he was quite popular among his paper route customers because he was never late and always respectful of people and property. He was rewarded handsomely every Christmas with gifts and bonus checks from the folks on his route. But he also had a bit of scallywag in him, sort of a hybrid of Tom Sawyer, the Artful Dodger, and Eddie Haskell.

For example, there was the time that Mrs. Walker's cat, Penelope, went missing. The 80-year-old spinster was at wit's end as to what to do, where to go, or whose help to seek out. She cried openly and often. One early morning on his route, Anthony stopped in front of her house to see Mrs. Walker standing in her yard alternating pleas of "Here, kitty, kitty," and "Come home, Penelope."

Young Anthony tried to console the inconsolable with a gentle hug and a comforting pat on the back from his bear paw hand. "Mrs. Walker, I will not rest until I find Penelope and bring her safely home to you. I have my route to complete, but when I'm finished, I will spend every free minute I have looking for her. I won't give up until I know she is with you!"

"Oh, Tony. My sweet Anthony…" as her voice trailed off into more tears.

Anthony was able to rest as soon as he got home. There was Penelope, wrapped in a blanket in a cardboard box tucked away in his parents' attic. Right where he left her three days prior. After two more days, Tony returned the cat to its owner and a celebration ensued! Mrs. Walker was beside herself with joy. She offered Tony cookies, juice, a slice of homemade cheesecake, a big glass of chocolate milk and a reward. Yes, money. Fifty dollars to be exact in crisp, new five-dollar bills.

"I can't, I shouldn't," Tony protested as he stuffed the bills into his jeans' pocket.

Word spread throughout the neighborhood about Tony's heroics. Little treats started showing up in the newspaper boxes for him, and not just at Christmas. He became the go to guy for helping families along his route with all manner of problems — and not just missing pets, although there were a few more before he stopped lest anyone get suspicious.

He became the South Frankfort fixer and fixer is what he would grow up to be.

His passion for reading helped get him through high school and college. But even then, he was a student of larceny more than arts and letters. He was 13 when Operation BOPTROT rocked Frankfort — Kentucky's state capital, or the city in a ditch as most people know it. BOPTROT was an FBI sting operation that brought indictments against 15 Kentucky legislators, including the Speaker of the House, and three civilians all on various corruption charges. One of them was a distant relative of Anthony's, something like fourth cousin twice removed on his father's side, or some such nonsense.

He was fascinated by the case, not because of what they did, but why and how they got caught. After all, was a contribution in exchange for a vote really any different than a reward for returning a missing pet? (You might think the moral compass of the state was or is malfunctioning. You might be right. Of course, in defense of the Bluegrass state, one could do a search and replace and substitute any state capital to find just as much corruption, Baton Rouge, Montgomery, Tallahassee, Columbia — it doesn't matter. They're pretty much all the same.)

"We shall never change our political leaders
until we change the people who elect them.
Mark Skousem

"Absolute power corrupts absolutely."
John Ackon

Only three years earlier, Anthony's world was turned upside down when his beloved University of Kentucky Wildcats were marred by scandal in the basketball program. Allegations included cash payments to recruits, the infamous "hundred-dollar handshakes" among wealthy boosters and star players, and cheating on a college entrance exam.

As with BOPTROT, Anthony was intrigued with how the perpetrators got caught. Even as a pre-teen, he knew certain protocols might have prevented some of the problems, like don't send a six-foot white kid into an ACT exam to take the test for a 6' 8" black power forward — allegedly.

Cheating on an exam shouldn't be that difficult. He didn't have to do it to advance his own academic career, but he knew plenty of people who could use the help. As he grew older and more sophisticated in circumventing law and procedures, he had mastered the art of fake photo IDs, talent solicitation, and deal making.

It didn't matter if you were a blonde debutant or a black defensive tackle, Anthony could find someone smart enough to pass the exam for you and close enough in appearance to pass for a sibling. For $500, $100 of which went to the test-taker, Anthony could get you a passing grade. And it didn't matter what the test was: ACT, DAT, SAT, MCAT, DAT, GRE, GMAT, LSAT — yes, LSAT.

The fixer had a new round of ammunition for his gun.

Anthony plopped his large frame on the barstool adjacent to Jack Adams and ordered a draft beer with some pretzels. He started munching and started talking.

"Aren't you Jack Adams? All-state at Belfry, back up QB for the Cards?"

Anthony had never played football. The coaches tried desperately, albeit unsuccessfully, to get him signed up. At 6'5" and a lean 235, he could have played almost anywhere on either side of the ball, but he was more interested in profiting from games than playing them. Still, he followed sports like most Kentuckians, as a second religion. For some, as their only religion.

"Yeah," Jack muttered, still deep in thought about his future, or more specifically, a future without granddad's PIN number.

"I'm Tony Barrows," as he extended the bear paw. "In town for business. Normally in Frankfort fighting fires, if you know what I mean."

Jack had no idea what he meant, but he took Tony's hand and shook it.

"Jack, I don't meet celebrities very often. What say we get another round and find a table to chat? I've been following you since you threw for 38 touchdowns as a freshman in high school. My family won't believe I met Jack Adams!"

No matter how down, how desperate, or how despondent the man is, a quarterback can always rebound with a little bit of hero worship. Anthony appeared to be willing and able to provide the balm Jack needed. The three fingers of WT had been reduced to one. Why not?

The road to Jack's bourbon buzz epiphany was about to begin.

Chapter 3 — Mary Beth meets Bridget

1998 was a big year in Kentucky, especially regarding the two things diehard residents of the Bluegrass State love — basketball and politics, with the most important being basketball.

Tubby Smith took a team that, on paper, was outmanned and outgunned all the way to the NCAA Final Four, where the Cats spanked Utah to win its seventh national championship.

Later that same year, hall-of-fame pitcher Jim Bunning bested former UK team captain Scotty Baesler in a race for the U.S. Senate seat left open when Mr. Democrat, Wendell Ford, retired after distinguished careers in Frankfort and Washington.

The UK win was in March; Bunning's contest was in November. In between, there was another momentous occasion, at least for Mary Elizabeth Corrigan from the St. Matthews area of Louisville. It was the year that Mary Beth lost her virginity — twice.

The Corrigan's and O'Shea's vacationed together every year at the Redneck Riviera, Gulf Shores, Alabama. It started when Mary Beth was four, as was Bridget O'Shea. Bridget's brother, Tim, was a year younger.

Gene Corrigan and Kelly O'Shea both worked at the Ford Truck Plant assembling F-150s. Not only did the dads work together, both families lived on Richland Avenue, both attended Holy Spirit Catholic Church where both mothers volunteered for after-school programs. It was fun for a while, but as they got older, Mary Beth and Bridget both started to resent the Siamese twin families and longed for more and newer friends.

Mary Beth had already decided that this would be her last trip to Gulf Shores with the St. Matthews caravan. She was 18 now. Ready to start college. Ready to be a woman. Part of that required giving herself to a man, or at least that's what she thought. Tim O'Shea would be her conquest, her first love—which he was—and the "man" to deflower her. How romantic!

Two young lovers enjoying each other to the crashing of Gulf waves. They had kissed a time or two; even held hands when the parents weren't looking. He wasn't Adonis, but he wasn't as gangly and awkward as some of the other high school boys in the neighborhood. It would be him!

The parents left at 7:00 for a night out at Ribs and Reds. With a table full of barbecued baby-backs, kettles of giant shrimp, and enough sides to feed a third world nation, they would be gone for a while. If pitcher one of draft evolved into pitcher two or three, they would be gone for quite a while.

Bridget left right afterward for a long, solo walk on the beach. Her only comment before she walked out the door was, "Don't wait up."

They were alone. Even before they touched, raging hormones generated enough heat to test the air conditioner's capacity. They sat together on the couch pretending to watch television. If Nielsen had called at that very minute, neither would have been able to identify the program they were viewing.

Tim wasn't as awkward as other boys in the neighborhood, true, but he was plenty awkward as he nudged a little closer to Mary Beth. He almost belted her in the forehead when he extended his arm to wrap around her neck and shoulders.

Mary Beth was quite inexperienced, but far less awkward than her soon-to-be partner. She turned to look into his eyes and let her hand touch his thigh. He jumped just a little, but then regained his composure, as if he were ever composed, and started stroking her blonde hair that fell past her shoulders toward the bow that kept her bikini top in place.

"Oh, Tim," she cooed. "This can be so wonderful. So perfectly wonderful. Do you want me as much as I want you?"

His clumsiness suddenly gone, Tim leaned over and kissed Mary Beth, at the same time letting his hand slip down to the delicate bow, which was untied in a single stroke. Their lips never parted, except to let their tongues touch and explore each other — the mouth, the face, the neck…

He bent down to kiss and caress her breasts. They were not the buds he had noticed when MB roared into puberty. They were firm and perky and heaving with her every breath. She slid her hand up Tim's thigh under his trunks and onto his manhood, which was stiffening and growing warmer with every beat of his heart.

Mary Beth leaned back onto the arm of the fake leather sofa and pulled Tim closer and closer, struggling to get his trunks off as he faced an equal struggle in removing her bikini bottom. At last. The young lovers wore nothing but each other's stares. The kissing became more frantic; pupils dilated; breaths became short and loud.

As the passion progressed, Tim looked to the heavens, as if praying for a miracle — the miracle of lasting as long as possible.

It didn't work.

As Mary Beth gyrated to enjoy the power that was inside her, Tim let out a little whimper, an "Oh God," and then collapsed his full weight onto her.

"What the hell was that," she thought.

"That was wonderful," she said. Was it her? Was she expecting too much or something completely different? If this is what sex is like, why does everyone talk about it so much?

"You are beautiful. That was great," Tim said behind a reddening face. He knew that the experience ended way too early. He could hear the television now as a stark reminder. The car ad that was playing when her hand touched his thigh was still playing. He thought, "please, dear God, let that be a sixty-second commercial."

Tim pulled on his trunks and pushed himself out of the sofa. He made his way to the door where he grabbed his wind jacket and said to no one in particular, even though Mary Beth was the only one there, "I'm going to the pier for pizza. Can I bring some back for you?"

As an afterthought, "Or would you like to go?"

That's the closest he came to eye contact in 10 minutes. They had held each other on the couch for a while, both pretending the evening's events had measured about a 7 on the Richter Scale. Both knowing that it was measured in fractions of that.

Tim couldn't get out of there fast enough. He was relieved when Mary Beth declined his invitation to join him for a trip to the pier. As soon as she said, "No thanks, I think I'll take a shower," he was gone.

Mary Beth let the hot water surround her. The steam wrapped her like blanket, warming her, caressing her, touching her every fiber. Was a steamy hot shower better than sex? If the past 20 minutes is any indication, perhaps so.

She emerged from the shower, stumbling in the fog to find her towel.

"Here," came a single word from the Good Samaritan who helped wrap the terry cloth around her. It was Bridget.

"So, how was it," Bridget inquired. "How did my little brother perform?"

Mary Beth was taken aback; she hadn't expected Bridget home this soon and certainly had no idea she knew about the sofa secret.

The overhead fan started pushing the steam out of the bathroom. Mary Beth saw that Bridget was standing only inches away from her dressed in a robe and nothing else. Probably waiting for her turn in the shower.

"Was he everything you had hoped for on this special night?" It was almost a taunt because somehow Bridget knew about the brief, oh so brief, dalliance.

"It was good," a response Mary Beth made more in defense of the action rather than affirmation of its existence.

"You want good? Follow me," Bridget turned and walked toward one of the bedrooms in the Gulf-front rental. Any bedroom would do, so she picked the closest — Tim's.

Mary Beth didn't know what to say, what to do, but she followed Bridget into the bedroom.

"Listen, MB, I want to show you something; I want to teach you something; but you have to be willing and you can't tell anyone."

Mystery. Intrigue. Romance. What would it be?

Mary Beth nodded without realizing she was.

"Come here," Bridget requested, not ordered. Her voice was calm and compassionate. "Come here," she said again as she patted the mattress.

Mary Beth complied.

"First, let's get rid of that silly towel," as the pink fish and octopus were cast to the floor. Almost simultaneously, Bridget pulled off the robe to expose herself — her complete self — to Mary Beth.

Both young women sat on the bed, eyes fixed on each other, their bodies emancipated from all clothing, and all intimidation, worry or pressure.

Mary Beth was blossoming. Bridget had been in full bloom for some time. Raven black hair and piercing yet understanding green eyes. She avoided the sun even on trips to the Gulf. As a result, her skin was creamy across her well-proportioned body. Her lips were full and pouty — so unlike her natural persona, which was always pleasant and often curious.

This was one of those curious moments as she gazed at Mary Beth. The blonde hair and blue eyes from her Irish father masked the dark complexion she inherited from her Slovenian mother. Unless you saw her as Bridget did right now. The golden glow of her skin stopped where the bikini started, revealing breasts that were as creamy white as hers.

"He's a boy," Bridget said apologizing for her brother. "He may be a man someday, but why wait? I can offer you the sensation you need, the sensation you deserve."

With that, Bridget cupped one hand on Mary Beth's breast and reached to caress her hair and neck with the other. Mary Beth did not resist. Bridget pulled her closer, still massaging her breast, and planted a firm kiss on her lips. Mary Beth, again, did not resist and, in fact, reached her tongue out to explore Bridget.

Bridget kissed Mary Beth in every way possible. On the lips, the neck, the breasts, her abdomen. MB's body was writhing in excruciating enjoyment.

In harmony, they moaned in ultimate delight. In harmony, they twisted, turned, and contorted their bodies until, in harmony, they exploded with an orgasm that belied their youth.

They fell into each other's arms. They fell onto the mattress as one. They fell asleep holding tight to each other's supple, naked bodies. They fell from God's grace as soon as their devout Catholic parents discovered them.

Chapter 4 — That Moment When You See Your Whole Life

"Ladies and gentlemen, we will begin boarding Flight 668 to Lexington in about 10 minutes..."

The rest of the announcement tailed off into nothingness as Jack Adams stared at his iPhone hitting refresh on his email again and again waiting to hear from Mary Beth. The cheap suit sitting next to him had ordered another Scotch, aka brandy. He offered to top off Jack's bourbon in hopes of engaging him in a deeper conversation. He knew they were both attorneys, from Kentucky, headed to Lexington, but that's about as much as he could drag out of Jack, who was and continued to be fixated on his phone. So he resigned himself to nurse his Scotch/brandy alone all the while watching Jack refresh his email.

It came.

Jack did a half turn away from his bar mate and read...

"Jack, this is bad. I don't know what to do, but we need to do something and soon. Here are the links. Let me know what you're thinking. Miss you. MB."

Jack placed a trembling finger on the first link that exploded with a headline from the Lexington *Herald-Leader*:

FBI Probe Expands to Frankfort Lobbyists

"Oh, shit"

The second link took him to the Louisville *Courier Journal*.

Sources Say Arrests Likely in FBI Sting

"Oh, fuck"

The third from Pure Politics quoted unnamed sources giving up the names of lobbying firms being investigated by the feds for allegedly initiating a vote buying scheme that made BOPTROT look like kids ripping off CDs at Walmart.

There was a fourth link, a fifth, a sixth. Jack didn't need to read them. He couldn't turn his eyes away from the Pure Politics story that outed the firms under investigation. From his perspective, one name was far more prominent than the others—Barrows and Adams Strategic Solutions.

The words screamed at him! How did this happen? How did everything get so far out of hand?

At that moment, the phone rang. Mary Beth.

"Jack, what are we going to do?"

"Get in touch with Tony ASAP. Make sure you're on a secure line. Find out what the hell is going on and where we stand in this nightmare. I'm getting on a plane in five minutes. Pick me up at Blue Grass in about an hour. We need to meet. In person. All three of us. Tell Tony there are no ifs, ands or buts. We meet at his place in Frankfort 20 minutes after I land."

"Got it, Jack. I'm scared. So scared."

"Tony can fix this. That's what he does. Don't fret sweetie. Don't fret. Tony can fix this."

Jack's words were meant to calm and console Mary Beth. He didn't believe them. This is something even Tony couldn't fix, or if he could, he would need more luck than a Powerball winner.

"I'll see you in an hour, MB."

"I'll be waiting for you, Jack."

Passengers were already boarding. The grandparents, drug store cowboy, and forlorn businessman were already making their way down the ramp to the plane. The mouse ears were in front of Jack, along with their parents. Dad was still glued to his phone checking race results and wishing he had bet the three horse in the seventh instead of the longshot. In front of them were the spring breakers, including one who obviously had failed to discover the protective properties of sunscreen. Right behind him were the tweens still chattering about which Mr. Right was the hottest. Bringing up the rear was the attorney who killed the last dram of his "brandy," fixed his combover and marched onto the plane.

As the door shut and the plane started pushing back, Jack got a text from Mary Beth.

"Tony says the sun will come out tomorrow."

Jack was used to Tony speaking in code. It seems like that's all the three of them had done for months. This was a good sign. Tony apparently had found a way to fix their mounting problems. At least that's what he hoped the message meant. Were the situation more dire, the message would have been dark and foreboding — though still in code. Jack was convinced Tony had a book of quotes he trotted out to communicate with MB and him.

No matter. He breathed an uneasy sigh and punched a response into the phone.

"Message received. See you in an hour."

Jack put the phone in airplane mode and closed his eyes. He wouldn't sleep, couldn't if he wanted to. But the darkness gave him a little peace. He opened them long enough to fumble through his briefcase to find ear buds. He wasn't really listening to music, but no one else knew that. Conversation with a stranger was the furthest thing from this mind. With his eyes shut and the engines lulling him, Jack relaxed more than he had in weeks. Still, his mind raced over what had happened and, more importantly, what could happen. How did a skinny kid from Belfry, Kentucky become the poster boy for political corruption in arguably the most corrupt state in the country?

The past is the past, Jack told himself. It can't be undone. But Tony would get them out of this mess. Tony was the fixer and nothing had ever needed fixing more than Barrows and Adams Strategic Solutions.

The minutes passed slowly. Jack checked his watch. It was the same time as it was when Mary Beth had called. The battery was dead. Time stood still — if only!

The captain squawked something unintelligible over the intercom. Below him, Jack could see the familiar trademark fences of Calumet Farm. The plane would touch down any minute. He knew Mary Beth would be waiting for him. Twenty minutes after setting foot on Kentucky soil, he'll sit with Tony in Frankfort at 1 PP.

Did he have a solution? Can the fixer still work his magic? In 20 minutes, MB and Jack both would know.

Chapter 5 — How to pass the LSAT

The drinks Jack and Tony shared so many years ago proved productive. Ever the scammer, Tony figured out a way for Jack's LSAT to be taken by a near lookalike with an IQ of 156, degrees in both chemistry and history, a Masters thesis in the works and the need for a little money to feed his drug habit. Uppers to stay awake and alert while studying, testing, and partying; downers coaxing his eyes to close for some much-needed rest.

Jack was game and obviously had no trouble coming up with the cash. But there was a problem. It was too late in the year to enroll for the fall semester even if he passed the LSAT next time it was given. He had already missed the June date; the next wouldn't be until September, which did not fit in with granddad's deadline to get off the payroll.

Tony fixed that problem, too.

"You can do me a favor in return for helping with this little issue you're having with your grandfather," Tony had a twinkle in his eye and a grin that was angelic and devilish all at the same time. "You can work for me."

With that, Tony reached into his pocket and emerged with a business card — something he had failed to do in the 45 minutes the pair had shared over domestic draft and Wild Turkey.

Barrows Strategic Solutions shouted in bold, gaudy letters. Beneath it read, "government affairs counsel." There was a phone number, an email but no physical address.

Jack wondered aloud, "What is Barrows Strategic Solutions?"

"Jackie, my boy, I create solutions for those in the business of government who have problems," the grin reemerged. "In some cases, I create the problem so that I can get paid to offer a solution. I'm a lobbyist. A purveyor of power for legislators and those who require their assistance. A resource for the Governor's office to keep a pulse on voter opinions. A champion of public policy for whoever is willing to pay for my contacts and services. In other words, I'm a political whore."

Jack had politics in his gene pool, but had never been actively engaged. That would all change by the end of his fourth tumbler of Turkey. Jack was about to become an associate with Barrows Strategic Solutions.

It was perfect. Tony would pay him $50,000 a year to be Jack Adams, all-state QB from Belfry, a "vital" part of the Cardinal football team and a celebrity to be trotted out like a Saddlebed in the show ring.

He, or more specifically, his doppelganger, would take the LSAT in September. He would make application to the Brandeis College of Law and enroll next August. Even better, Tony offered to keep him on payroll while he was in law school, help get him ready for the bar exam, and then up the ante for him to stay on for a minimum of five years.

Perfect! Walking around money — really good walking around money. Granddad off his back. Mom giving up hopes of his return to Pike County. The talent pool of lovely women in Louisville at his disposal. And guaranteed employment for as long as he wanted it. He had no clue as to what he would be doing, but he really didn't care.

"Tony, I don't know you, but I like you. You are fixing a problem for me and I appreciate it. I'm going to take you up on this right here and right now. That's not the Turkey gobbling! Call it fate or blind faith, but I'm in."

With that, Tony raised his glass for a toast.

"We have a deal?"

Jack responded in kind, "We have a deal."

Tony was almost giddy when the waitress, who had been more than flirtatious the entire time she was serving them, brought the check.

"I'll take care of this, Jack. You take care of her!"

When the waitress returned, Tony gave her a credit card; Jack gave her his number written on a cocktail napkin.

She leaned over Jack's shoulder pressing her ample breasts into his back.

"I get off at 6:00," she whispered.

"Then we'll both get off by 7:30," Jack winked.

He followed her with his eyes as she wriggled back toward the bar.

Jack showed his own devilish grin, "I think I'm going to like being a political whore."

Chapter 6 — Repent you sinners

The afterglow Mary Beth and Bridget enjoyed in slumber was shattered with a loud and piercing, "OH MY GOD!"

The source was never determined. Mrs. Corrigan? Mrs. O'Shea? It didn't matter. Startled from their deep sleep, Mary Beth and Bridget shot straight up in bed, realized that they were as naked in front of their parents as they were at birth, and struggled frantically to find a towel, a robe, a sheet — anything to cover themselves.

Mr. O'Shea spoke, or rather screamed, first. "What in the hell is going on here? What are you two doing?"

From that point on, it was a series of rapid fire comments, questions, and cries in agony.

"My God, my God. What is this?"

"You two get dressed now, and then we'll talk."

"It's a sin!"

"What possessed you?"

"How long has this been going on?"

"Oh my, God. Right under our noses. Sinners living in our house."

"Do you know what you're doing; what you're putting us through?"

"How dare you touch my daughter."

And then, sudden silence. From everyone. The Hatfields and McCoys, or that should be the Corrigans and O'Sheas, looked at each other for what seemed like an eternity. In fact, though, it was mere seconds before the bickering between the two families resumed.

Bridget was being accused of something vile and sinister in "touching" Mary Beth, who was obviously perplexed because the sex was consensual: she tried to interject, but was quickly silenced by both families.

The newly sanctioned feud rivaled an orchestral crescendo; words become more inflammatory; the faces redder; the blood pressure higher; and the finger pointing more animated than a Disney cartoon.

"Pack your things NOW!" Gene and Kelly screamed it almost simultaneously. The mothers consoled each other as best they could, but nothing would help, nothing at all.

The girl's bolted down the hall making every attempt to cover themselves as they fled from their judgmental parents. Still, a generous portion of each's backside was exposed as they ran right by Tim O'Shea, who returned from his solo pizza party at a most inopportune time.

He drank in as much as possible to figure out what was going on, but his analysis was distracted when he caught sight of the fleeing fannies. Thoughts started racing through his head that weren't exactly puritan, but they were quickly disintegrated when his father grabbed him by the arm and marched him to the room where Bridget sought sanctuary.

"You stand here and protect your sister," as if she needed protecting. "I'm going to pull the car around to load up. We're out of here. The sooner the better."

"But dad, it's late...."

Tim never had a chance to finish the sentence. Kelly turned on his heels and went flying through the screen door, paying no attention to the groans it made as it slammed shut.

In a similar vein, Gene raced to the Corrigan family car as quickly as he could, barking orders over his shoulder for his wife and daughter to be packed and ready to leave in 10 minutes.

No other words were exchanged. None. No one spoke. Eye contact was avoided, except between Mary Beth and Bridget. How had this night of mutual exploration between two consenting young ladies transformed into a night of explosive anger? What did the parents not get about the simple fact that two women could enjoy each other beyond trading recipes at a book club?

Bridget wasn't the aggressor, rather the instructor. Mary Beth wasn't a victim as much as an apprentice. They both exuded a sensuality that would sustain them in future relationships — and there would be many for both with men *and* women. Wise beyond their years; mature beyond their years; sexual beings beyond their years; that was Bridget and Mary Beth.

The cars scattered gravel as they sped away from the "scene of the crime." Both fathers were driving faster than they should. Both mothers crying uncontrollably. Both girls sat quietly and relived the ecstasy they had enjoyed. Tim? Well, Tim sat quietly as well, replaying the brief encounter with Mary Beth, and projecting on the screen in his mind the two young, firm, and bubbly behinds running to their rooms.

The 10-hour drive back to Louisville would be torture — for all!

Richland Avenue would never be the same. The Ford Truck Plant would never be the same. Holy Spirit Church would never be the same. The details of the ugly incident were never discussed with friends in Louisville, but it was clear to all who knew them that the conjoined families had been separated.

There might as well have been a wall dividing the two clans like the one that divided Berlin. Gene and Kelly put in for transfers to new departments, or new shifts. The mothers both resigned their positions at the preschool. Father Victor signed letters of transfer for each family — one to Holy Trinity and one to St. James.

The parents would never again speak to each other as the blame game lived on.

Bridget and Mary Beth didn't seem to care. They would escape to each other's rooms when the parents weren't home or meet for mocha and a make-out session at Starbucks. The sex continued as passionately as it was in Gulf Shores and as frequently as they could.

Mary Beth also felt pity for Tim and tried to reassure him that his 40-yard sprint could be a mattress marathon with the right amount of encouragement. She offered as much help as she could, with Tim as the willing student. With apologies to Bob Seger, she used him, he used her, but neither one cared. They were getting their share.

The wedge was still driven between the family patriarchs. The friendship would never be restored. Mores the pity because they had long since given up on any sort of congenial, much less carnal, relationships with their wives. The "children" all moved out of their respective houses later that fall into pursuits of their own.

After completing two years at Louisville's Catholic college, Bellarmine University, Bridget was accepted at UC Berkeley and moved to California as fast as she could where her lifestyle would be more readily accepted.

Mary Beth evacuated the mother ship on Richland Avenue that same fall, accepting a scholarship offer from the University of Charleston because of her prowess with a palette and brush. That would eventually open new doors for her in Frankfort — doors that led to the glitz and glamor of government relations and a lasting friendship with Tony Barrows.

Tim? Tim abandoned all hope of being a successful lady's man once he and Mary Beth parted ways. After reexamining his life, his skills, his ambition, and his future, Tim became Father Timothy. His escapades with Mary Beth would be but a memory to relive during particularly boring confessions. For Gene and Kelly, this was their personal vindication from the vility that plagued Richland Avenue. Both of their daughters had promulgated scandal on their houses, their church, their families. Tim may not atone for all of the Corrigan-O'Shea transgressions, but it was a start.

"Bless me Father, for I have sinned."

Chapter 7 — Ichabod Crane

When Big Tony was still delivering papers, he already was developing a strong dislike for Stuart Carroll. Stuart also had a paper route, but he was different. Tony was ever the scallywag, Stuart was the saint. Tony was a flimflam man — just ask Mrs. Walker's cat, Penelope. Stuart was a boy scout — not a real boy scout because he refused to be content with one good deed daily.

Oh, and Stuart disliked Tony; mutual malevolence.

The south side of Frankfort belonged to Big Tony. Stuart knew that and never crossed the bridge — any of the bridges. Stuart couldn't lay claim to the north side, either, because he failed to intimidate, display any leadership, develop a following, or even come out of his house to engage with others in his neighborhood. Stuart was an island in the cesspool of Frankfort politics.

But, damn he was a good writer. Or should that be was and is.

Stuart went from delivering newspapers to writing for them, first at Franklin County High School, then the *Kentucky Kernel* — the student newspaper at UK, a brief stint with the nearby *Winchester Sun*, and then the bigtime, the *State Journal* in his hometown covering all things politic in Frankfort and Washington a mere three years after getting his journalism degree from UK.

It was with the *Kernel* that Stuart also honed his skills as an investigative reporter able to disarm interviewees with his stumbling style, develop leads from confidential informants, and slam the hammer when the time was right. He won a student journalism award at the state level for his exposé on sexual misconduct allegations against a group of interns at the medical center. A year later, he received national attention for his report on unethical lobbying practices by a UK vendor trying to expand its reach into other state colleges.

It was only a matter of time before his diligence and investigative prowess would land him a Pulitzer—or so he thought. It seems survival would take precedence over salutations. That became abundantly clear on his first day as a member of the capital press corps.

After picking up his credentials at the Legislative Research Commission office, he found his way to the cubbyhole and little desk that would be his to file reports on legislative, gubernatorial, and political activities. One problem. His desk was occupied—by Tony Barrows.

Stuart was Ichabod Crane to Tony's Brom Bones. Big Tony had at least nine inches and 85 pounds on poor Stuart. The intimidation that started so many years ago at the pick-up point for their newspaper routes continued all through high school with a respite during college when they chose different schools. But now...

There he sat—all 6'5" of him—with his feet propped on what was supposed to be Stuart's desk, reading the *State Journal's* latest edition which he lowered when he heard approaching footsteps.

"Well looky here," Tony said never offering to remove his feet from the desk. "If it isn't my old buddy, Stuart. I hear congrats are in order, so I'm here to offer mine."

With that, Tony unfolded from the chair and slowly rose to tower over the cowering Mr. Carroll. The big bear paw went out and smothered Stuart's hand in an exchange of pleasantries.

Stuart was speechless; Tony was not.

"Listen buddy," Tony whispered. "I'm going to tell you something right here and right now. If you *ever* come close to investigating me or one of my clients, there will be hell to pay. That is not a threat; it's a promise. And unless you have a tape rolling right now, which I seriously doubt, I will deny that we ever spoke, and certainly deny ever threatening you. Got it, buddy?"

Buddy is a name Stuart would hear a lot in the halls of the capitol and in legislative offices across the way in the Annex.

"I'll get that information to you as soon as possible, buddy."

"Buddy, I have no idea why that legislation failed."

"You know, buddy, if you can get the Speaker on the record, you'll have a great quote for your story."

"Buddy, our contract awards are fair, impartial and follow the letter of the law."

But there was something sinister about the way Tony said the word. Maybe it was the timbre of his voice. Maybe it was the look in his eyes that drilled a hole through to Stuart's soul. Maybe it was just a little, healthy paranoia.

After seconds, which seemed like hours passed, Tony spoke again.

"Buddy, if you ever need the real scoop on what's going on in this hellhole, I'm your man. But if you ever turn attention to me..."

He may have repeated the threat; he may have altered it in some way. Stuart couldn't hear the jumble of words because right now, he was focused on not wetting himself. Tony had literally scared the piss out of him.

When the big man started walking away, Stuart made a beeline for the men's room. There was no mouse's room in the capitol.

After relieving himself, Stuart settled into his little cubicle and opened a virgin journal. The first ink that touched its snow-white pages said simply:

"December 15. First day on the job in the capitol. Encountered Anthony Barrows. Will follow up with research on him and his clients as soon as practical. Stay tuned."

Unlike the fictional Ichabod Crane, Stuart Carroll was here to stay, and buddy, Tony Barrows would learn that — not as quickly as Stuart would like, but he would learn it.

Chapter 8 — Buddy of a different variety

College was a blur for Mary Beth. Charleston presented ample opportunities to hone her skills on canvas and in bed. She excelled in portraits — charcoal sketches, pen and ink, water color, oil — virtually any medium available to her. She also excelled in refining her sensuality.

Sex appeal didn't adequately define her attributes. She was a classic beauty in the mode of Grace Kelly, Audrey Hepburn, Ann Margaret, and Sophia Loren. She dripped with sensuality — but she was not tawdry in her attire, her manner, or her demeanor. Like it or not, Gene Corrigan's little girl was the very embodiment of a sexual and sensual being.

Ask Dr. Forester, the art professor who taught her sculpture and succumbed to her Aphrodite beauty.

Ask Hannah Moncrieff, the Boston debutante who brought her liberal concepts of sex and a noticeable accent to Charleston. She and Mary Beth were inseparable for six months before her parents got her accepted at Hahvud.

Ask Will Preston, who teetered on the brink of engagement before he learned that many of his brethren in Sigma Alpha Epsilon had the same amorous experience with MB — some more than he.

Ask yourself why a woman so beautiful, so sensual, so sexy, so enlightened would be so engaged in frequent and meaningless trysts with men and women. She wasn't a victim of abuse. She had never experienced any measure of self-loathing. She was not compensating for a lack of social acceptance.

Simply put, she was on this planet to arouse and please—others as well as herself.

One companion she would come to know and love as a brother as much as anything else was Tony Barrows.

Her uncle—the only family member on her mother's side still talking with her after the Bridget episode—was a political whore just like Tony. The whores were in abundance in Frankfort attempting to pass bad legislation for their clients and kill good bills that would cost those being represented a shilling or two. He used his contacts and client list to get Mary Beth a summer internship with LRC—the Legislative Research Commission. Her job essentially was working to provide administrative support to the House Labor and Industry Committee. It was there that she met Big Tony. His client was the Kentucky Automobile Workers Union, which had a vested interest in repealing the state's Right to Work legislation. Subject matter for a future discussion.

They first met in Tony's office—the cafeteria in the Capitol Annex. She was with her mentor, Jane Hupman—a lifer at LRC and a fixture on any discussion of labor policy. As MB scanned the crowded cafeteria for a seat, Jane pointed to vacant chairs right next to Tony.

Pleasantries were exchanged as Jane dived into her chicken wrap. Tony was fixated on Mary Beth. The din around him was barely audible. Legislators, staffers, lobbyists, and media hacks passed by him like lines in the center of a highway. He knew they were there, but paid no attention.

Likewise, Mary Beth was fixated on Tony. This is the first time since her Gulf Shores experience with Bridget that she was not in charge. He dominated with his mere presence. She wanted him — there and now, but sex on the salad bar probably would have led to trouble.

After lunch, a different story. The two made conversation as they walked through the Annex tunnel to the underground parking garage. Tony escorted her to the black Suburban that bore his name on the license plate — Big T. Together, they went for a ride, but never left the parking garage.

She used him, he used her, but neither one cared. They were getting their share.

Once the internship ended, Mary Beth was offered a full-time job with LRC as a staffer for the Labor and Industry Committee due in part to the great work she had done during her internship, and due in part to the frequent hand jobs she provided for the LRC director, whose third marriage was quickly disintegrating.

As a full-time employee, MB was eligible for the annual rating of "sexiest staffer" by the other political whores who frequented the capitol and annex. After year one, there was no contest. Mary Beth was the clear winner, as she was in years two through four before the head letch among the lobbyists suggested that they "retire her jersey." No one woman could ever evoke the strong feelings of lust that she did. Nor could they set hearts aflame as she did. Mary Beth was in a class by herself. It was unfair to have others compete.

Before Tony and Mary Beth strolled to the Suburban for a round of meaningless sex, Jack Adams was introduced as the newest associate for Barrows Strategic Solutions. Ever the rounder, Jack made comments about MB in hopes that his first score in the capitol would be with someone so mysterious and sensual. She wasn't playing along.

Undeterred, Jack kept coming back for more opportunities to talk with her, laugh with her and flirt with her. He had gotten the greenlight from Tony. His lust had been satiated. It was Jack's turn.

They met for a drink at Serafini's. He hadn't been this intimated by a girl since Rosa Lynn Selby in middle school. She hadn't been this nervous since she and Bridget shared sensations that others only dream about.

Across Broadway from Serafini's is the old capitol building — now a museum in homage to Kentucky's political past. Behind the building is an alcove with blind spots to the street and neighboring properties. Mary Beth sipped her vodka and tonic; Jack inhaled his Maker's Mark. Someone, and neither recalls which one, suggested that they move the party to the old annex.

If only cameras had been rolling, the two could have made a mint in the adult entertainment market. Soft pecks became more voracious with each passing minute. While the kissing continued, the hands started to explore. Her skirt went up, his pants went down. Basked in the setting sun and the long shadows it cast, the two reached a climax that they had only dreamed about.

As the breathing slowed and the blood flowed more evenly throughout their entire bodies, MB and Jack both thought about a repeat performance at some point in the future.

It didn't take long. The next day, it was a vacant office in the annex. Two days later, an encounter at the best — no, the only — Chinese restaurant in town. A week later at the Frankfort County Club on hole number seven — a par five with lots of trees to the right of the fairway.

Jack and Mary Beth became fuck buddies. They would pursue other relationships, lure others to their bed for a night of pleasure, and keep their radar on high alert for Mr. or Ms. Right. But whenever the mood struck one or the other, a night of gratuitous sex followed with no regrets from either party.

Mary Beth was sex personified.

Jack was sex personified.

Together, they were the ultimate sexual power couple, and others started to notice — including Stuart Carroll who was attempting to connect dots leading from Tony to Jack to MB to the chairman of the House Labor and Industry Committee, and ultimately, to the Governor's Mansion.

"Buddy, can you believe what is about to happen?"

Chapter 9 — Who can you trust?

As the plane slowed to a crawl on the runway, Jack fired up his cell phone.

"I'm here."

Mary Beth's response was equally terse, "Out front. Black 640."

As is the case with most deplaning, the line inched forward at a snail's pace. Not what Jack wanted.

One of the girls in the princess gown and mouse ears was sound asleep. As the frantic mother tried to rouse her, dad turned his attention to his cell phone and the latest race results. Theirs would not be a happy homecoming.

Slowly, ever so slowly, his traveling companions made their way to the front of the plane and onto the ramp. Jack had no luggage to claim, only the briefcase that he carried constantly like a security blanket.

As he exited the ramp and hit the long corridor to the gate, Jack passed by the others as quickly as Mine That Bird did in the 2009 Derby, only there was no joyous waving of the crop like Calvin Borel had done. Quite the contrary. Jack had his head down, peering over his Ray Bans toward the escalator, out the front door, and into the BMW Mary Beth had waiting for him.

In one fluid motion, he kissed her, she kissed him, he started punching in numbers on his phone, she found drive on the gear shift and left the curb with tires squealing.

"Slow down," Jack commanded. "We have enough shit going on; we don't need a speeding ticket."

Mary Beth complied.

No one answered Jack's call. He tried a different number with the same results. Then he dialed a third number.

"This is Clement Combs. I can't come to the phone right now…"

"FUCK. Where is everybody?"

One last attempt at talking with a human being — 502-564-2611.

"Good afternoon, Governor Lyon's office."

"Lisa, it's Jack. I need to speak with the Governor — now!"

The voice on the other end of the phone grew hushed.

"Can't, Jack. He's in the with the FBI and Attorney General."

"Jimmy? Is he around," Jack asked about the Chief of Staff.

"He said he was going to Antonio's for an early dinner of beer and pizza."

Lisa thought it odd; Jack knew the code. Jimmy Flannery, the COS, was on his way to Big Tony's.

"What about Shaughnessy? Have you seen him today?"

The ever-vigilant Lisa had been keeping watch on the Governor's office for three years. She knew the power brokers and the wannabes. She knew Riley Shaughnessy from his days as a volunteer on the Lyons for Governor Campaign and, more recently, as the man who single-handedly leveraged his union contacts to get repeal of right to work on the legislative agenda. She also knew that Shaughnessy was nowhere to be found.

"Nothing, Jack. The only people coming into the office today are the AG, the fibbees, the First Lady, and a gaggle of reporters, who I turned away."

Bless her heart. She wasn't a receptionist, she was a pit bull. The reporters knew better than to piss her off, so they obeyed her command and cleared the office. They were still outside, pacing on the marble floors in the rotunda, but they were not *in* the office where they might catch a glimpse of the FBI special agents.

"Let me know if you hear anything after the meeting."

"Will do, Jack. This will all end well. I know it will."

Lisa's words offered little relief for Jack.

After he laid the phone down, silence took over. A long and deafening silence. The state-of-the-art sound system was mute. Neither one of their phones squeaked with an incoming call or text. Jack and Mary Beth stared straight ahead counting down the miles and minutes until they would be at Tony's house.

Once they cleared Versailles, there were no stoplights to slow the journey to Frankfort. MB was careful not to exceed the speed limit—at least not by much. She wasn't sure why she remembered it and why she thought it amusing at the moment, but she recalled a state trooper advising her about pushing the limits of speeding. "Nine you're fine, ten you're mine."

The speedometer would not exceed 64.

Twenty minutes after they pulled out of the airport, just as Jack had said, they were at Tony's house situated on a cliff over-looking the Kentucky River. The car hadn't come to a complete stop when Jack threw open the door and marched as quickly as he could to the porch. Tony was waiting.

He motioned Jack into his great room with Mary Beth close behind. Shaughnessy was there. So was Flannery. There also were a couple of gubernatorial minions whose names escaped Jack. They had been part of the scheme to advance the Governor's legislative agenda. Now, they would be part of the solution to the shit storm brewing in the capitol, or at least that is what Jack was hoping.

On the island separating the great room and kitchen was a bottle of Maker's—half empty. Jack suspected that Tony and the others had a head start on him. He and MB would catch up quickly. Life's problems seem much more manageable with some 90-proof bourbon coursing through your veins.

"Were you followed," Tony asked.

"Of course I was followed," came the curt response. "What do you think this is? Law and Order? The bad guys elude the good guys? Christ, Tony, get in our reality. We have the full weight of the Justice Department, the FBI, the KBI and the Attorney General's office crashing down on us! It's not your job to worry about whether 'we're being followed,' but to fix the damn problem. That's what you do, right? Then fix the damn problem NOW."

The room fell quiet—deathly quiet. One of the minions reached into the ice bucket to freshen his drink and was greeted with looks that could kill from everyone else.

Mary Beth broke the uncomfortable silence, "It's almost 6:30. We need to turn on the news."

Tony had a wall of televisions in his house — eight in all so that he could watch multiple football and basketball games during betting season. But the programming now had nothing to do with covering a point spread.

WHAS was the first to report an FBI investigation that could reach all the way into the Governor's office and to the Speaker of the House.

WKYT was next. Then WLEX, WDRB, WLKY and on and on until every television outlet in Louisville and Lexington reported the news — all attributed to a special investigative report by the Frankfort *State Journal* and a reporter named Stuart Carroll.

Shaughnessy was not just a political whore, he was a media whore who subscribed to every news service known to mankind — real or fake. Between commercials for a car dealer and fast food restaurant, he got a text message from CNN.

"Whistle blower threatens to take down Kentucky government leaders."

A flick of the remotes and all eight televisions were dialed in to CNN doing a live interview from Frankfort with Stuart Carroll.

"To recap," said the news reader, "sources confirm that a Justice Department investigation is underway in Kentucky. Targets of the investigation reportedly are Governor Damien Lyons, several members of his staff, and legislative leadership including the Speaker of the House. More after this…"

How could there be more?

With a click of the master remote, all of the TVs went black.

Like lemmings marching to the sea, those watching the news moved as one to the deck overlooking the river. The sun was setting on Tony's old Kentucky home.

Shaughnessy's phone pinged again.

"U.S. Attorneys from the Eastern and Western districts of Kentucky have scheduled a joint news conference at the federal building in Frankfort at 8:00."

This is going to be a long night.

Chapter 10 — It all started...

They say a journey of a thousand miles begins with a single step. They also say that the road to hell is paved with good intentions. The journey that Jack and Mary Beth were on started innocently enough. Who would have ever thought it could all go wrong — so terribly wrong? They would find themselves in their own hell soon enough.

Jack and Tony had been making quite a name for themselves in the lobbying arena — so much so, that their firm topped some older and more established operations in billings within three years after Jack became a political whore and less than one year after he became a named partner with Barrows and Adams Strategic Solutions.

The pharma industry called. The ophthalmologists called. The tort reform advocates and tort reform opponents both called. They became proponents of whatever position their clients took, and they did it well thanks in large part to Tony's relationship with the Senate president and Jack's hero-worshiping Speaker of the House. Both came from rural parts of the state; the President was a Republican; the Speaker a Democrat. Both also learned that the fine art of compromise still worked in a state, a country, more polarized now than at any time in history.

It worked on pension reform.

It worked on tax reform.

It worked on legislation for public-private partnerships.

It even worked on a tort reform package that the doctors and the trial lawyers could agree on.

But there was no movement toward compromise to repeal right to work. Like most of the states in the south and industrial Midwest, right to work legislation sailed through the Kentucky legislature only three years prior to Jack and Tony being engaged by a consortium of labor unions hellbent on repealing it.

For a decade or more, labor groups in Kentucky and elsewhere were losing their stature, their status, and their power in political matters.

Riley Shaughnessy was the golden boy who was going to turn the ship. He had the argument, but needed an audience with decisionmakers who could help sell the concept. He retained Barrows and Adams. They in turn brought him President Offutt, Speaker Patrick, and Jimmy Flannery, the newly elected governor's chief of staff.

It was really a pretty simple compromise. The open shops would be closed again. Anyone working for a company represented by a union would have to pay their dues to the labor guys, which guts right to work. *However,* if they didn't want to participate in a union's political activities, that portion of their dues would go into a special fund to support spouses and children of union members who were killed on the job or who suffered a debilitating accident or injury.

The bookkeeping would be clean. Every member would pay the same amount in dues, which brought a little political clout back to labor.

From a public relations standpoint, it was golden. Labor would undergo a rebirth and have compassion as the focal point to justify the new stature. The commercials backing the initiative and the legislators who supported it would tear at heartstrings from Pikeville to Paducah—an old expression used often in Kentucky politics to symbolize widespread support from Jack's hometown in the east all the way to Paducah near the convergence of the Ohio and Mississippi rivers in the west.

What no one knew was that the new law would also include a provision to establish a fixed amount for overhead and administration. You probably have heard about charities that rip off donors by spending most of the money raised on overhead and expenses. No different here. Unions would be allowed to set an O&A fee at 75 percent. Yep. For every dollar in dues paid into the widow(er)s' and orphans' fund, only a quarter would wind up benefiting anyone except the unions.

No one knew about that "compromise" arrangement. If they did, the bill—any bill even remotely related to repeal of RTW— was dead on arrival. That didn't concern Riley, nor Jack, nor Tony, nor Mary Beth who would be the eyes and ears on members of the Labor and Industry Committee.

Here is a quick civics lesson on the legislative process in Kentucky, and likely elsewhere. It is a little more complicated than "I'm just a bill" from Schoolhouse Rock.

Let's say a bill starts in the House, like the repeal effort will do. It has to clear a committee—in this case, the Labor and Industry Committee that Mary Beth controlled from her position as a lead staff member, and the one woman in LRC who could make grown men *and* women weak with impure thoughts.

If it passes in committee, it goes to the full House. If it passes there, it is sent to the Senate where it is assigned to a committee for approval and then on to the full Senate. If the House and Senate versions are the same, it is then sent on to the Governor for his signature, and Governor Lyons was eager to put pen to paper on this one.

If the two versions are different, it would go to what is called a free conference committee where anything could happen — and often does. That is what Shaughnessy hoped for; keep the intricacies of the bill below the radar and media scrutiny until it was delivered to the Governor for his signature after the conference committee.

It was a complicated plan, but that is why he retained Jack and Tony. He only wanted the best. Their $25,000 monthly retainer included plenty for them and plenty to spread around as need be. Riley only needed assurances from three people other than Jack and Tony to set his plan in motion:

Senate President Larry Offutt.

House Speaker Teddy Patrick.

Governor Damien Lyons, or more specifically, COS Jimmy Flannery.

It started at the Frankfort Country Club with a fundraising golf scramble. No one seemed to be able to recall the charity. It didn't matter.

Jack rode in a cart with the House Speaker; Tony was with President Offutt. Flannery was in the clubhouse schmoozing the crowd with Mary Beth close by to be his eye candy for the afternoon. Shaughnessy was in a cart making the rounds to greet legislators, lobbyists, and renowned socialites. He wasn't alone. Riding with him were two scantily clad beer maids who would offer weary golfers a cold drink on a hot day. Melissa and Melanie. One blonde, one redhead. Both stacked thanks to the kindness of their neighborhood plastic surgeon. Both wearing a bikini top to reveal their endowed chests and Daisy Dukes to showcase long, lean, and luscious legs.

Riley's first stop was where Tony Barrows and Jack Adams were loosening up with their guests.

After some quick introductions, Melissa and Melanie poured drinks for the foursome. Water for Jack; beer for Tony. And bourbon—10-year-old bourbon on ice—for Offutt and Patrick. Somehow in the pour, some of the corn-based elixir spilled on Melanie's chest and went streaming toward her exposed navel.

Melissa would have none of it; no 10-year-old bourbon would be lost in the netherworld beneath the Daisy Duke waistband. She licked the bourbon from Melanie's body—just above the waistband, past her rock-hard stomach and up through her heaving breasts to her lips, where they shared a brief taste of the spillage.

Offutt and Patrick could barely contain themselves.

Shaughnessy spoke once the girls' lips had separated.

"You know, it's still 15 minutes before we start. Would any of you gentlemen like Melissa or Melanie to kiss your balls for good luck?"

He didn't mean their Titleist's.

In a scramble, every foursome starts at a different hole.

They had drawn number seven; par five; lots of trees to the right, which is exactly where the most powerful men in the legislature would point a golf cart with Melissa and Melanie wriggling on their laps.

Who knows what their golf game would look like, but they were about to get lucky.

Back at the tee box, Tony, Riley, and Jack toasted to a successful launch of their plan. The tiny microphones positioned in the watch pocket of the Daisy Duke jeans would capture everything they needed for stage one.

Meanwhile, at the clubhouse, Mary Beth was making sure that Jimmy Flannery was completely onboard with the strategy, which she outlined for him on a window in the sauna. One wonders if the steam was generated by the hot rocks, or by Flannery himself. It didn't matter. The plan was solid. He knew it. He now had to convince his boss, the Governor, of that fact.

Mary Beth swiped the glass with her hand to erase the schematic. Jimmy watched in wild wonder at the vision before him.

"Fore," he said suggestively as he approached her nubile body. He pressed himself against her, which in turn pressed her breasts onto the steamy glass. "What say we make a little steam of our own? I'm game for your plan if you're game for a little action."

With that, he pressed harder against Mary Beth.

This was not the time. This was not the place. And Jimmy Flannery was not the at all what MB saw as a companion in any way, shape or form. She swung her elbow around and caught him in the jaw sending him collapsing onto a bench.

Taken aback by her refusal to accept his advances, Flannery wrapped himself in a towel and stormed to the showers.

"You'll be sorry, bitch. I'm the Governor's Chief of Staff."

"You'll be sorry, asshole. The mightier they are, the harder they fall and it could be squarely on your pin head."

Mary Beth took a seat on the bench that bore a little blood from a cut on Flannery's head. Calmly, she retrieved her phone from the pocket of a robe that Flannery had stripped from her.

She clicked the off button; rewound the digital recording to make sure she had sound; and then texted Jack.

"My part is done. The first floor will be on board. I want a shower first and then catch up with a real man. Know anyone?"

Jack laughed aloud.

"My place. Tonight at 8:00. I'll cook. Bring your toothbrush."

At just that moment, the golf cart with Melissa and Melanie as co-pilots returned from the woods. They hopped off, gave their fellow travelers a peck on the cheek and jumped into the beer cart with Riley.

"See you again on number 13," cooed Melissa. "That is, of course, if you're ready."

The men let out hardy guffaws,

"We'll be ready," Offutt assured them. "We will be more than ready!"

The girls drove off with Riley. Offutt turned to Big Tony.

"Where the hell can we score some Viagra right now?"

Tony, the fixer, unzipped one of the side pockets of his golf bag. It was better stocked than a small-town pharmacy. Pills to keep you partying; pills to ease your pain; pills to relax you, excite you, and sustain you. And there was a bottle of little blue pills that Tony opened for his golfing partners.

"If you take this on number nine, you'll be primed and ready by the time we hit thirteen."

Laughter all around.

As each man in the foursome addressed his own tee shot, different thoughts raced through their minds. Offutt and Patrick could see nothing other than Melissa and Melanie offering themselves again. Tony saw nothing but stacks and stacks of hundred-dollar bills surrounding him at a beach house on the Gulf. Jack saw Mary Beth — relaxing on his balcony sipping a cold vodka and tonic while he served up a hot ribeye.

What none of them realized is that while Offutt and Patrick were recording extramarital conquests or while Melissa and Melanie were recording those who were participants of the tryst in trees that might be necessary to leverage a vote, or while Jack, Tony and Riley were toasting each other, there were two parabolic microphones picking up every word they said.

One belonged to the FBI; the other belonged to Stuart Carroll.

Chapter 11 — Pin ups and smack downs

When Mary Beth decided to stay on at LRC rather than return to Charleston, it broke her parents' hearts. She would have been the first college graduate on either side of the Corrigan clan and, as their only child, that dream would be dashed forever.

She didn't care.

The relationship she had with her folks was strained at best, bordering on completely broken. It all stemmed from their reaction — no, their overreaction in Gulf Shores when she was found with Bridget. Besides, if she ever wanted to go back to college, she only needed nine credit hours in her major to get a BFA.

After that one summer as an intern for the Labor and Industry Committee, and the flings with Jack and Tony, she realized she was more interested in the art of creating power rather than the power of creating art, although she was good at both.

Tony noticed it first. One day when she joined him at his office — the Annex cafeteria — she took a sketch pad from her bag and started doodling while patrons passed by with their lunch trays in hand. She could capture their inner self in the seconds it took for them to come into view and leave her sight. The depressed expression as seen through a blank stare, wild wonder in the giggles of college interns — not unlike herself, the furrowed brow of a legislator as concerned about his liaisons as much as he was his legislation, the sexy secretary looking around frantically for a strategic seat near a power broker.

She captured it all and with the childlike innocence that made so many Norman Rockwell paintings icons of Americana.

But she also had a wicked side, as Tony found out when he pressed her about her work. She flipped through several pages to another set of sketches: women in sexy poses wearing sexy lingerie, sexy bikinis, or nothing more than their own sexy bodies. Norman Rockwell had left the building. This was pure Alberto Vargas—the legendary artist who made the pin up an art form with his work in *Esquire* and *Playboy*. Google it and prepare to be impressed.

"You're really good at this, MB. And I know nothing about art! But I do know we can use this to help build our base."

We?

Build *our* base?

Was Tony including her as part of the Barrows Strategic Services family?

"I'm going to ask you a really dumb question, but I'm just a dumb kid from south Frankfort. Can you draw from a picture? I mean, can you use a picture instead of a model to do a portrait?"

"Of course." She responded with a bit of uncertainty in her voice.

"And what about real people? Can you put them in a pose like this even if they're not there?"

"Probably. These were taken from memories of girls on the beach or in the sauna. I just removed some clothing and substituted other things."

"I have a meeting in 15 minutes with Bill Kerr..."

"The House Labor Chairman," she interrupted.

"You're coming with me. I'll explain on the way. Come on, and bring that pad with you."

On the slow elevator ride from the basement of the Annex to the third floor, Big Tony explained the life and times of Bill Kerr.

"Retired electrician and union steward.

"In the legislature for 16 years, 10 as either the chairman or ranking Democrat of Labor and Industry. That means we need him in our pocket.

"He has two loves in his life; okay, one love and a lust. His granddaughter Ashley is the light of his life. Talks about her every chance he gets. He has a picture of her on the wall behind his desk. Study it. Memorize it. Then draw her in a Norman Rockwell setting. You make it up, but make it cute and funny. Can you do that?"

"No problem. Color or black and white?"

"You pick. The object of his lust is Amber, his secretary. He has been banging her for months now. Can you do one of those sexy poses with her as the model?"

"It won't be exact because I can't see any birthmarks or tattoos or anything like that if she has on clothes, which I'm sure she will. But I can get it close."

"Great," Tony was beside himself. These would be great gifts for Rep. Kerr: one he could share with his wife, his daughter, son-in-law, and, of course, Ashley. The other he would share only with Amber. Since Tony was registered as a lobbyist, he couldn't do gifts like this, but MB could — a staffer doing a nice thing for one of her bosses.

Mary Beth didn't understand why this was a big deal to Tony, but she didn't mind. She loved to draw and this provided her a temporary outlet. As it turned out, when Tony was finished running out the string on his new "service," Mary Beth would find it to be a far cry from temporary or part-time.

1 PP. We've all seen enough television dramas to know that it's One Police Plaza, headquarters for the NYPD. In Frankfort, the address meant something quite different: One Palace on the Palisades. Tony's house.

It was palatial, and it stood high above the Kentucky River on the Palisades, a stretch of limestone cliffs, caves and springs that stretched for more than 100 river miles from Madison to Franklin counties.

Tony's house enjoyed more than a great view. Business had been good and was getting better. There were 6,500 sq. ft. on three levels with decks on each overlooking the river and the capitol building in the distance.

The first floor was his primary living area: gourmet kitchen even though he didn't cook, comfortable leather couches and chairs—Chesterfield type like the ones Tom Selleck had in the 1 PP of *Blue Bloods*, and an entertainment area with a wall of eight HD televisions, a state of the art sound system, and pool table salvaged from the old neighborhood when Monson's Billiard Emporium closed. There were two bedrooms—the master and a guest room that both dripped in luxury.

The basement was party central. A full kitchen, wet bar, two "recreation" rooms that had queen-sized beds layered with 800-thread count Egyptian cotton sheets, plush towels for the shower and Jacuzzi in each room, and a stocked minifridge and pantry that included a fishbowl full of condoms and a bubble gum machine that dispensed Viagra. These rooms were for his guests as well.

Upstairs were two other guest rooms and a second master suite. This would be Mary Beth's home. Why not? It saved her on rent because Tony let her stay for free. After the initial dalliance in the Suburban, Tony was content to be a mentor, an advisor, a big brother. He was also her muse — not so much by inspiration as by insistence.

He fitted the two guestrooms upstairs with studio lighting, props, clothing… anything Mary Beth needed to do her thing. Both rooms had great natural light as well with big windows overlooking Tony' personal three-hole golf course in his front yard.

One of the rooms was naughty — the one where Mary Beth drew her best replicas of the Varga girls from ladies that Tony would supply her.

One was nice with lots of pastel colors, murals on the walls, and the embodiment of a childhood innocence she had forgotten about when she turned 16.

Mary Beth was happy with her studios — plural. She could continue to develop her art in exchange for free rent, and nothing more. Oh occasionally, Jack would show up unannounced, or linger after a party had ended in order to make sure the thrill they enjoyed had not vanished.

When Mary Beth finished a sketch or painting, Tony would give it to his target as a gift from an appreciative MB for the opportunity to be a part of the legislative team working in the best interest of Kentuckians. She choked every time she heard him say it because it was far from being anywhere close to true.

Tony would also have a duplicate made and framed for his home: Norman Rockwell on the first floor; Alberto Vargas in the basement. He was building quite a collection of MB's sketches and paintings, which meant he was also building a great deal of favor in the House and Senate because of the portraits of their loves and lusts.

There was the occasional hiccup—like the time Governor Lyons came out to 1 PP for billiards and bourbon. When the Pappy started getting low, Tony suggested they move downstairs to take in the setting sun and crack open a new bottle on the deck below.

On the way from the bar to the deck, one of the troopers in the Governor's detail caught sight of a Vargas replica that stopped him in his tracks. It was his wife clad only in a string of pearls.

"What the hell!"

He made a beeline for Tony and reached for his neck. Tony swatted away the trooper's hand with his bear paw at the same time the Governor lunged forward.

"Landrum, stand down. Stand down now!"

The trooper stepped back. His blood pressure was rising by the second. The Governor was breathless as he tried to interject calm. After the brief adrenaline rush, Tony was nonplused.

"Sorry, Sergeant Landrum," Tony said. He was crafting a story as he spoke. "She had my friend paint this as a surprise for *you*. It wasn't supposed to go up on the wall. We are nothing if not discreet."

The blood pressure started to lower.

"I'll have my housekeeper take it down immediately."

The pressure lowered more — now 140 over 110.

"Please don't get me wrong Sergeant, but you are a lucky man."

What he didn't say was that Maureen, the trooper's wife, was more interested in giving something to Tony than to her husband. It didn't matter. 125 over 95. Things were almost normal.

"Let me get you a drink. Governor? Okay if Sergeant Landrum has a drink?"

"Max, you've earned it."

The ice crackled as a pour from the new bottle of Pappy splashed down on it.

"Here Sergeant. Enjoy the drink and the view."

He sipped the bourbon. He looked out over the Palisades. He thought about his wife; then he thought about Flannery, who was there, too. He needed some company now to console him. 800-thread count sheets were calling his name.

The camera and microphone Tony had placed in the room would give him negotiating leverage. He liked leverage. It would also give MB her first opportunity to immortalize guy on guy sex in one of her paintings.

Fore.

Chapter 12 — The hills are alive

1 PP was earning a reputation among Frankfort insiders as being a rich hunting ground. There were always plenty of women — bikini clad by the pool in summer and around the hot tub in winter. Since Mary Beth's jersey was retired as sexiest staffer, Tony and Jack made it a point to befriend the annual queen and her court — the runners up. They were welcome anytime — even had the security code to get in if Tony wasn't around. They would bring their girlfriends for an afternoon of gossip around the pool, or sneak in a rendezvous with someone who wasn't their husbands or boyfriends.

The bar was always amply stocked.

The stash in the fridge and pantry meant they wouldn't go hungry.

But there were no drugs — Tony's one and only rule. His golf bag stash was different. That was always off campus. At 1 PP, a different moral yardstick. Have a great time, enjoy yourselves, *mi casa su casa*, but absolutely no drugs. Not weed. Not coke, Certainly not opioids. And if there was any evidence found of meth or heroin, Tony himself would throw you over the deck into the murky waters below.

He wasn't kidding.

Never any arguments, except from Jack who did love a line of cocaine every now and then. He was the exception Tony made, but never in the house. Either on the deck or in a golf cart far down the par four fairway.

Whenever Tony hosted a gathering of dignitaries and wannabes, it never failed. Jack would ask him for a bourbon and coke. Tony knew that meant a bottle of bourbon and a ride in the golf cart for a snort—usually with no worse than a third runner up in the staffer competition.

The only other chemical exception Tony made was with the magic blue pill so many legislators and lobbyists required to meet the expectations of their latest conquests. That's why they were readily available in gumball machines. One such patron was Labor Committee Chairman, Bill Kerr.

After Mary Beth finished her version of the chairman's granddaughter, Ashley, she went about the delightful task of making Amber look like a Varga girl. When she got close to finishing, Tony called Amber for an appointment to see Chairman Kerr.

Amber greeted them with a smile, announced their arrival and shimmied to the coffee machine to make a cup for each guest. They had barely finished their first sip when Kerr threw the door open and bellowed, "Tony Barrows as I live and breathe. So good to see you again. And my favorite LRC professional Mary Elizabeth Corrigan! Come in. Come in."

The animated greeting was for show in case a constituent was nearby or waiting in the anteroom of his cavernous office.

He closed the door behind him, giving Amber a quick wink in the process. Kerr motioned his guest to chairs around small conference table.

"Well, Tony. What now? What dragons are you trying to slay?"

"Why Chairman Kerr, suh, I do declayh I know not of what you speak."

The Southern accent was crucified, but they all got a laugh from it.

"Seriously, Bill, we're here to give, not receive."

With that, he passed over a gift wrapped in pink tissue paper with a delicate green bow.

"You know, Tony, there is a rule about receiving gifts from lobbyists."

"Which is why the gift is from Mary Beth."

He smiled with that assurance and tore off the tissue.

"Oh my. Oh my. It's Ashley. How did you... Oh, this is beautiful."

He was admiring his granddaughter in a pose from a Rockwell print. "First trip to the beauty shop." She had the same crop of red hair, the same wide-eyed wonderment as the little girl Rockwell had drawn, but it was unmistakably Ashley.

"This is grand. This is just grand," as he propped the frame on its easel and set it on the table. "I will look at this every day with so much appreciation."

He meant it.

"MB, did you do this? What talent! I'm going to show everyone who comes in my office."

He meant that, too.

Tony allowed the chairman a few more moments of total adoration of the painting and then offered a second package wrapped in bright red paper with a black and white striped bow.

"This is really too much..." he stopped short interrupting himself with, "Oh my God."

Before him was Amber the Varga girl. She was lying on a love seat with one leg hanging over the back and the other trying to escape the spiked heel that rested on the floor. A striking red boa covered the sensitive areas, but Kerr knew what and where they were.

"How did you? Did she pose? Of course not. I would have been there? How did...Oh my God."

The leer lingered a while longer before Tony pointed to a delicate charm bracelet around the arm that kept the boa strategically placed between her legs.

"See Mr. Chairman. The charms are really numbers. 7-2-6-3-3. That's the security code to my house. Use it anytime you'd like. I'm sure you and Amber will enjoy the views."

Tony and Mary Beth had barely cleared the door when Kerr picked up his phone and dialed his wife back in Ashland.

"Honey, you won't believe what a staff member just gave me. It's a painting of Ashley. So cute. Looks like Norman Rockwell himself painted it. I'll bring it home this weekend to show you, but after that, it stays in my office. So cute!"

The whole time he was talking with the dowdy Mrs. Kerr, he was actually laser-focused on the shapely Amber, rubbing his zipper as he drank in every delicious inch of the painting.

"Love you, too," he said quickly to end the call. And then he buzzed Amber.

"Have one of the interns cover for you this afternoon. I have something very special to show you. I'm going out the back way. Meet me in the garage in 10 minutes."

Before he left, he grabbed a can of La Croix from the fridge in his office and used it to wash down a blue pill he had removed from his desk drawer. If his timing was right, the magic would start working within a few minutes after he entered the code to 1 PP and downed a stiff drink with his assistant.

Amber was prompt. She always is. Kerr had already tucked the picture away in his trunk to show her later. He nearly ran over a visitor as he backed out, lowered the window, and apologized. The aggrieved party made note of his license plate as he drove off just in case a personal injury lawyer was roaming the garage. No such luck,

In Kentucky, legislators get special plates for their vehicles. For example, S-15 is the state senator representing the 15th Senate District. H-22 would be a house member representing the 22nd House District. Kerr's plate was H-69. How appropriate for the afternoon he had planned.

The 20-minute drive to 1 PP was uneventful, which is always good when you're a 66-year-old man with a 32-year-old knock out. He punched in the code on the gate and then used the same code to enter the house. Easy.

He had Amber go in first because he had "forgotten something in the car."

"Pour us a drink, baby. Tony's bar is loaded. I'll have a Blanton's. You treat yourself to whatever you little heart desires."

Amber scooted toward the bar; Kerr retrieved the painting from the car; as she spun around to hand him his drink, he held up the painting.

"That's me," Amber was shocked. "But how could it be? I love it, Billy. I really like it. How did you…"

She leaped at him spilling a bit of the bourbon in the process and planted a huge kiss on his lips.

He stepped back. Studied her. Studied the painting. Studied her again.

"I think you're a little overdressed," he laughed.

"We can fix that," as she kicked off her heels and slowly unbuttoned the tunic top she was wearing.

"Oh, the look on your face! I wish I had captured it on video."

They locked arms and clumsily tried to undress each other as they made their way to the leather sofa that peered out onto the deck and the scenery that completed the canvas.

He didn't have to capture her surprise on video. Others did it for him — from houses in the lower rent district across the river.

One camera rolling belonged to the FBI; the other was being manned by Jerry Duncan, a friend of Stuart Carroll's.

Chapter 13 — A good time will be had by all

1 PP was not a brothel. Tony Barrows was not a pimp. He just liked to please his guests and that often required a little creative thinking. For example, when Melissa and Melanie came to say goodbye to the legislative dignitaries that Tony and Jack were entertaining at the golf event, they had a roll of five $100 bills tucked in their cleavage. Offutt and Patrick were invited to go "bobbing for Benjamins," a phrase Tony coined of the spot.

They looked at the girls and then at Tony and back at the girls.

"I hate losing a game to you," Tony winked. "But a bet's a bet."

This was the cover they needed to avoid a breach of ethics. A bet is a bet. Nothing illegal about a friendly Nassau on the golf course.

The two legislators dived willingly into the crowded bikini tops and emerged with the bills between their teeth. They peeled off two of the bills and gave them to Melissa and Melanie as a tip for the service — the beer cart service — they had performed. The M&M girls caught the whole thing with their digital recorders still wedged in the front pocket of their shorts.

It wasn't long before Tony and Jack started losing all sorts of bets. Most were in the $200-$500 range depending on where the winner ranked in the legislative pecking order. All went smoothly, with the exception of Senator Clayton Schilling's embarrassment. As he bobbed for the Benjamins, Juliet picked just that moment to squeeze her breasts together for a little more fullness. Schilling came up empty, but Juliet had a full set of dentures — upper and lower — clinging to her chest. That was the lone hiccup.

As the two pioneers had done previously, part of the winnings was shared with the buxom hostesses, who made bobbing for Benjamins doubly entertaining, or double D entertaining. You pick. And each of the hostesses carried a recording device to catch the play by play, although hiding spots were sometimes difficult to find. Jack and Tony were collecting quite an arsenal of information.

There also was the putting game Tony used it to bet on with legislators at his personal 1 PP golf course. Granted, it wasn't PGA quality, but it was sufficiently tough to challenge the weekend warriors on Capitol Hill.

There was a long par four heading from the tee located just outside the pool, along the cliff with a slight dogleg left. If a player pushed the drive to the right side of the fairway, the ball was out of bounds; way out of bounds plinking in the water some 100 feet below.

The second was a par three deceptively long because it was up hill. The real challenge, though, was the undulating green that tested the most proficient putter.

The third hole was an easy par five back down the hill, straight as an arrow with a big, welcoming green to finish.

It was back at the second where Tony created another friendly betting opportunity for his guests. The putting surface was tricky and difficult to read because of breaks and turns. It was also the furthest spot away from the house and any onlookers who might spoil the fun.

First up, Larry Grider, who was chairman of the Senate Labor Committee — another key contact for Jack and Tony. He fashioned himself as a good golfer, but admitted that number two would be a challenge.

"Let me make it just a little easier for you," Tony said with the wry grin he was wearing more and more often.

With that, he motioned to the pin attendant, Josie. On cue, Josie dropped the pin, then dropped her shorts and sat spread eagle behind the cup; her legs acting as a funnel to the hole.

"If you can get it close enough with Josie's help, I'll consider it a win for you. A bet's a bet."

Grider could hardly concentrate with Josie's lady parts winking at him, but he stroked the ball, watched it roll through a break, catch Josie on her right knee and follow up her thigh to the cup.

"Birdie for you, bad for me," boomed Tony. "Josie, pay the man."

She bounced up, replaced her white cotton shorts, and made a beeline for Grider. She stuck her tongue in his ear, her left hand in his pocket with the Benjamins in tow, and her right hand down the front of his pants.

"Nice putter, Senator," she said in her best Marilyn Monroe impression.

As she turned to retrieve the flag, he gave her a pat on her round, firm behind and promised to be back in the future for more putting games.

A good time would be had by all if Tony had anything to say about it. Shaughnessy kept him in prize money. The legislators became accustomed to good food, strong drink, and shapely women. All with complete discretion.

And relationships were forged. Yes, Tony and Jack benefitted; but so did some of the overworked and underpaid girls who supplemented their income as hostesses for Barrows and Adams. One actually wound up marrying a freshman legislator from Western Kentucky who was fresh off a divorce. That's also where Chairman Kerr first met Amber—the green on number two. She was able to leave a dead-end waitressing job for the steady state salary and health insurance afforded her as Kerr's administrative assistant. She also enjoyed his continued generosity for a job well done.

Tony the matchmaker! Hardly. The only matches he cared about were legislators and votes. He and Jack were getting close to having enough leverage to start their bill through the maze that is the General Assembly.

Two major obstacles stood in their way. One was Senate Majority Leader, Darren Peavler, who wrapped himself tightly in the Tea Party agenda and offered no indication that he could be moved. As far as he was concerned, any repeal of RTW was DOA. Mary Beth will work on that.

The other was the Lieutenant Governor, Tamara Looney. Yes, the people of Kentucky elected a Looney to the number two position in the state. She kept her maiden name rather than be Tamara Tunie so as not to be confused with the actress. She considered a hyphenated surname, but that would make her Looney-Tunie—good for Warner Brothers' cartoons, not for a rising star in the Democratic constellation.

Despite the comedic name, she was a ballbuster and no admirer of her boss, Damien Lyons. (And yes, the Republicans had a field day during the election with what they referred to as the Lyin'-Looney ticket.)

She had no legislative authority or influence. In fact, she had pissed off more legislators than she had won over. But she was a media darling and media coverage is not what Barrows and Adams needed. Most others involved in the long-term strategy could simply deflect coverage or ignore reporter inquiries.

Not Tamara. She would use the same commanding voice that had served her and her clients so well in the courtroom to shout her concerns from the mountaintop. This is a bill that needed to progress quietly, eke out a close vote in the House and Senate before heading to the conference committee. If they did their jobs correctly, Jack and Tony wouldn't read one word about it in the newspaper until it had cleared conference and landed on the Governor's desk for his signature.

Tamara Looney would be a problem.

She had Stuart Carroll on speed dial and he had her number programmed as well.

Stuart spent more time in her office than he did his own.

She had populated her staff with loyalists — not party loyalists, but Looney loyalists.

Tamara Looney *would* be a problem. Tony had to figure out how to fix it. Little did he know that his nemesis Stuart, and Stuart's new best friend, Special Agent Rachel Whitney, would come to his "rescue."

Chapter 14—What did the Governor know, and when did he know it?

Minutes passed ever so slowly. Jack looked down at his watch again. Damn. Same time it was when he left Atlanta. The battery hadn't healed itself.

Not for Flannery. His phone started pinging with all manner of alerts from Kentucky news outlets. Tony took his cue from the phones.

"It's almost 8:00. Turn the TVs back on."

As minions one and two struggled with the elaborate remote system, Mary Beth lost all patience, stripped the devices out of their hands and lit up the eight screens in front of them. A few minutes remained before the scheduled news conference, but all of the stations were running crawls—you know, the words crossing the bottom of the screen for special announcements, like an approaching storm. This was to be a storm unlike any other.

It looked like a Hollywood opening as lights scanned across the concrete façade of the John C. Watts Federal Courthouse in Frankfort. While the collected crowd buzzed in anticipation, Tony and company cracked open their third bottle of Maker's and started passing it around. Leslye Pratt from WLEX was the first to break the television silence. MB switched all of the TVs to 18 News. Tony toasted the news reader—an alumnus of 1 PP—and thought to himself, at least she'll be fair, a delusion that lasted only a few seconds.

"Tom, Myra, in just moments, U.S. Attorneys from Kentucky's Eastern and Western Districts will stand at this podium..." dramatic turn of the head and shoulder "...for an unusual joint press conference regarding federal grand jury investigations in Louisville, Lexington, and here in Frankfort. We are told that the grand juries have been meeting since last November exploring allegations of government corruption and tonight, have handed up sealed indictments. Because they are sealed, we don't know how many have been accused, who they are or the nature of the allegations."

The camera zoomed past her blonde hair to the podium where four people gathered.

"What the hell is she doing there?" Tony screamed as he had never screamed before.

'She' was Tamara Looney, Lieutenant Governor, liar, Judas, and working undercover for the FBI's latest sting.

Tony hurled his double old-fashion at the screens setting off an explosion of glass and bourbon as one TV fizzled to black. The other seven were still lit and staring with unblinking eyes at Tony, Jack, Mary Beth, and the island of misfit boys at 1 PP.

"I'm Attorney General Robert Breckinridge and I have the unfortunate task of laying out the basics of a long and in-depth investigation by the FBI, the KBI in my office, and various other law enforcement agencies. Together, we have unearthed a trail of alleged government corruption that leads all the way to the Capitol."

Anyone knowledgeable of the capitol floor plan knows the only office holders who call the dome home are, the AG and Lt. Governor, both of whom were at the press conference, Clarence Nolan, the doddering Secretary of State whose only brush with corruption came in the 1980s when someone gave him a free ride to an out-of-state conference, and, the *big and*, Governor Damien Lyons. How was he involved? What was the nature of the corruption? Why could reporters not find him or Flannery? How long had he been involved in whatever this nightmare was? Allegedly.

AG Breckinridge continued.

"Joining me tonight are Stan Duncan and Karen Wilson, U.S. Attorneys from Eastern and Western Districts of Kentucky who helped guide the investigation, which has resulted in 47 sealed indictments being handed up tonight by the three grand juries impaneled in Louisville, Lexington and Frankfort.

"Also joining us is Lt. Governor Tamara Looney whose office played a pivotal role in exposing the breadth and depth of the corruption being alleged."

Tony fired a second bourbon bomb at a misfortunate wide screen,

"Damn her. Damn her soul to hell!"

Minions one and two looked at each other in disbelief. They had unwittingly helped set the snare that would trap themselves and dozens of others. Minion two started crying.

Shaughnessy joined Tony in his own curse-fest. Flannery plopped down in an overstuffed leather chair with three fingers of bourbon and said nothing.

Chapter 15 — The prodigal prize returns

Since they had left for college, neither Mary Beth nor Bridget thought much about each other. It's true that in the first few weeks after Bridget left for California, they did exchange a few phone calls or drop each other a note by email. Both realized, however, that maintaining any sort of relationship like the one they hoped for — completely carnal — could not be satiated by phone sex with an entire continent separating them from the intimacy they both desired.

That changed one sunny summer morning in Frankfort of all places. Mary Beth was staffing a Labor and Industry Committee meeting in the interim period between legislative sessions. When she looked up from her laptop, there was Bridget looking as ravishing as ever — skin still pure, creamy white, green eyes still lighting up the room, and the raven hair that framed her face — a different do, but unmistakably, Bridget.

Their eyes met at the same time causing both to bolt their heads in disbelief and mouth in unison, "Oh my God!

The questions raced through MB's mind like flash cards.

When? Why? What for? How long?

Was she back in Mary Beth's life for keeps?

As soon as the chairman adjourned the meeting, the two ran to each other and embraced — as friends, not as long-lost lovers. That would come later.

They stepped back, looked at each other, still in misbelief, and hugged again.

"Bridget, I can't believe it's you. You haven't changed a bit, except to get more beautiful."

Bridget was equally effusive with her compliments. Neither had a meeting until 2:00; time to catch up.

Arm in arm, they chatted and giggled like school girls as they flew down the stairs to the cafeteria for a cup of coffee. One wouldn't be enough. They had too many years to cover.

After the conversation had played out, Mary Beth knew:

Bridget tried acting after college, but gave up after a couple of years and came back to Louisville—the millennial mile along Bardstown Road.

Paralegal.

One those big firms with more names than necessary.

Worked for one of the hotshot senior partners.

New client needed representation on a manufacturing matter. That's why they were in Frankfort. (Mary Beth couldn't believe she was a staffer on the very committee Bridget's client needed.)

Love life? Tried guys. Tried girls. Tried both at the same time. "Nothing to match what we had."

Mary Beth's bedtime stories raced through her mind. Guys. Girls. Both. Nothing close—except maybe Jack. Bridget wasn't her first, brother Tim, or Father Timothy was. But she was the best. Better than Jack because she was as much concerned about Mary Beth as she was about herself—in every aspect of the lovemaking. Guys, or at least most guys including Jack, don't get it. A guttural moan, a whisper of "yes" that grew louder, and an orgasm, real or fake and most often fake, was all the guy needed to determine that 'My work here is done.' Roll over. Go to sleep.

That was Jack, too. Not Bridget.

Subconsciously, Mary Beth slid her hands across the table and laid them atop Bridget's. Their eyes met just as they had done so many years ago in Gulf Shores. Had there not been a cafeteria full of people, they would have taken each other right there on the table. Maybe they would anyway! Most of the passersby probably have sex with their spouses once a month and on special occasions — like a solar eclipse. They don't know passion the way Mary Beth and Bridget can display it. They don't know tenderness like the two can share with each other. They don't know the warm explosion of mutual satisfaction the two teens first enjoyed to the sounds of crashing waves.

Bridget turned her hands upward to take Mary Beth's and they both held tight. They stared in wonderment. Their pupils were dilating, and their breaths were getting shorter yet deeper. No words were spoken. None were needed. They were oblivious to the world. Until…

"Am I interrupting something?"

Chapter 16 — Friends like these

Tony loomed over the two as an adult would over children. Before he began the process of folding his massive frame onto one of the tiny chairs, he extended his giant bear paw and took Bridget's hand.

"Tony Barrows, friend of Mary Beth's. And you, lovely lady are…"

"Bridget O'Shea, another friend of MB's from the stone age."

"Tony, Bridget and I grew up in the same neighborhood. Our families were close. We even vacationed together. But that was eons ago."

By this time, Tony had bent and twisted his body onto one of the cheap, plastic chairs in the cafeteria.

"Well, friend of Mary Beth's, welcome to my office," at which point he swept his arms outward and upward. "Any friend of Mary Beth's is a friend of mine."

Tony sat attentively as the two continued to catch up on all that had transpired since they last spoke. Seven years had come and gone. Beyond the personal anecdotes, they realized that seven additional years of experimenting, exploring, and learning the fine art of sensual and sexual pleasure would make they black belts in the sport, if there were such a thing.

Occasionally, Tony would interject an "Uh huh," or let loose with one of his trademark boisterous laughs, but this time and this place belonged to Mary Beth and Bridget.

As they were about to say goodbye with promise to see each other again, soon, Bridget's phone pinged, which in itself was miraculous given how poor wireless signals are in the catacombs of the Annex basement.

"Change in plans. Client wants mtng t'mrw. U can take off. Meet me at the F'fort office at 9."

The judge just issued a pardon. Bridget didn't want to make the 2:00 anyway. Meetings between clients and attorneys tend to be way too long and way too boring—justification for more billable hours. This was wonderful news and, since Mary Beth could use some of the 'comp' time she had amassed, they could spend the afternoon together.

Tony wasn't even part of the good news, but that didn't stop him from reveling in it.

"This cafeteria serves really bad coffee, really bad food and has a really bad atmosphere for a reunion." With that, he pulled out his money clip, peeled off three $100 bills and handed them over to Mary Beth.

"Go to Serafini's on me. Eat and drink as much as you want. Much better place for old friends to catch up."

"But I really need to get back to Louisville and rest up for tomorrow," Bridget said with a note of dejection in her voice.

"Nonsense!" Tony said. He would make sure a good time was had by all.

"MB, when you all finish downtown, grab an Uber to 1 PP. Bridget can spend the night with us. No reason to cut the party short just to save a few minutes on the highway."

"Great idea, Tony." MB was ecstatic. "Bridget, can you? You must! I have plenty if clothes you can pick from for tomorrow. Please say you will."

"Of course she will," Tony insisted.

"Well, if it's no trouble," came the sheepish response. "I really would like to see more of Mary Beth. You never know when we'll hit another seven-year gap."

"It's done!" Tony was a living, breathing exclamation point by then. As he slowly, and clumsily came to his feet, he offered one more directive.

"Bridget, if I don't see you again, it was a pleasure to meet you. I have business tonight, so I may not be home. You and MB have a great time. That's an order."

As they both gave a little wave to their host, Mary Beth was thankful for a friend like Tony. She knew he would not be home so she would have more time with Bridget. From her perspective, Bridget knew she would see a lot more of Tony.

"1 PP," Bridget asked. "Stay with us? Home?"

"I'll explain it on the way downtown. Let's go!"

Chapter 17 — Plus one

Serafini's is the place to be seen by the political elite of Frankfort. Situated across from the Old Capitol and Annex in the heart of downtown Frankfort, it is the magnet for powerbrokers and pretenders to their thrones. The food is always good, the drinks devoid of added water, and the clientele connected. On this sunny Thursday afternoon, the only connection Bridget and Mary Beth cared about was with each other.

They took a table near the bar that was situated so that both could see the comings and goings of patrons through the front door. The afternoon was slow, as usual. During happy hour, the pace of patronage picked up. Fried oysters and bruschetta piqued their interest. So, too, did Ancient Ancient Age — the best kept secret among Kentucky bourbons, according to Jill, their waitress. Kentucky girls, Kentucky bourbon — of course.

Over the next four hours, they ate (working their way to the dinner menu by splitting a Bluegrass Salad and a Chicken Picatta pasta dish), and they drank. The Triple A was remarkably good, so they stayed the 10-year-old course.

They giggled; they nearly cried; they let out boisterous laughs that would rival Tony's; they spoke in hushed, but increasingly slurred tones so as not to be overheard. They fended off advances from young studs and moneyed seniors. They were in a world all their own.

After knocking back their fifth Triple A and soda — the last one compliments of the Senate Minority Leader — they determined the time had come to hail an Uber. Jill was happy when they departed, not that she didn't enjoy waiting on them, but for the $70 change back from their check that was left on the table for her.

While waiting on the Uber driver outside, MB pointed across Broadway to the Old Capitol.

"You know, there's an alcove behind there where you can't be easily spotted by anyone. Jack showed it to me."

Bridget looked puzzled.

"Oh, you don't know Jack. My bad. He's Tony's partner and my fuck buddy."

Bridget was silent.

"What the hell am I saying," MB chimed as she broke the uneasy silence. "Tonight is about two old friends—you and me. To hell with everybody else."

With that, the two kissed playfully as the Uber driver pulled to the corner of Broadway and the St. Clair Mall.

"1 PP and step on it," Mary Beth mumbled as they climbed into the ancient Toyota Camry.

"Oh, Tony's place," beamed the Kentucky State University student who had once partied with the powerful at that very location.

During the fifteen-minute drive from downtown to the Palisades, Bridget and Mary Beth started to get reacquainted. They gazed; they touched; they kissed; they fondled.

At one point, Mr. KSU nearly left the road, amazed by what he watched in the rear-view mirror.

"Careful, dude" Mary Beth chided. "You're hauling precious cargo."

It was the dark of the moon, no street lights and only the illumination of his high beams to guide him, as Mr. KSU inched along the access road to 1 PP. In the backseat, Mary Beth's and Bridget's "get reacquainted" session now involved tongues and exposed breasts. Again, he veered ever so closely to the edge of the road, jarring both women as he turned hard to his right to avoid the ditch.

"Listen, Junior, keep your eyes on the road and you'll get a nice tip. Sway a little more to the left, and we're all going on our last ride into river. Got it!"

Mary Beth had teetered on the edge of the cliff before with someone who was paying more attention to her than to the road. She would not have it again.

"Yes, ma'am. Got it."

When they finally entered the gate code and pulled into the circular driveway at 1 PP, Mary Beth said under her breath, "made it. Will miracles never cease?"

She punched in the payment information on her phone app and then looked in the mirror at the 20-something year-old driver.

"You know, given the show we put on back here, you ought to be paying us."

Mary Beth smiled; Bridget struggled desperately to contain herself.

"Yes, ma'am. How much? I only have about 30 bucks, but it's yours."

Both women exploded in laughter. Mary Beth extended $50 to the peeping Tom and asked, "how about one for the road?"

With that, she pulled Bridget close, reached out to her face with her lips and tongue to kiss the willing partner, caressed one of the exposed breasts and reached through the waistband of her skirt to the womanhood that lay beneath.

The driver struggled to maintain any semblance of composure. When Bridget and MB exited the Camry, they thanked him for the ride, he thanked them as well and they knew why. They headed to the front door; he sped off toward the gate. After it had closed behind him, he scanned his surroundings. No one in sight. Leaning back against the hood of the car, he successfully released the pressure that had been burning in his pants ever since they hit the East-West connector that led to Tony's. It didn't take long, not long at all. He almost exploded before the gun was out of its holster.

His roommate would never believe him. He didn't believe it himself. If this is what he could expect, he might just forget college take up Uber as a full-time job.

As soon as MB entered the code and walked in, motion sensors poured lighting over the great room, kitchen, dining area, and hallway leading to the bedrooms.

Neither Tony nor Mary Beth knew they would have a house guest, but you would never have known it to see the place. 1 PP had been cleaned from top to bottom by Marla and her crew of Bosnian expatriates. The pantry was full, and the bar had been restocked. The lights in the pool changed color to display a full rainbow—too slow to be disco, too fast to be an antique Christmas tree color wheel. The bigger spotlights were trained on the golf course and the nothingness beyond the barrier that separated dry land from the river some 10 floors down.

It was all theirs.

"Oh my God, this is where you live," was all that Bridget could muster. Mary Beth already had explained the living arrangement. She stayed with Tony—as friends and nothing more. No different than if Bridget were living with her brother, Tim, or Father Timothy. Everything strictly platonic. Mary Beth could do as she pleased; come and go as she pleased; and entertain houseguests as she pleased.

At this point in time, nothing would please her more than to rekindle the relationship she had enjoyed with Bridget so many years ago.

Mary Beth wobbled toward the bar and fixed both a nightcap—club soda with a twist. They did have to be able to function in the morning. She threw open the sliding door and stepped onto the pool deck. Bridget followed.

MB raised her glass and toasted "Here's to old friends. May we never part again."

Bridget followed suit with her glass raised high and her stares down low at the woman Mary Beth had become.

The drinks were tossed back. The clothes were tossed off. Bridget dived into the pool with Mary Beth close behind. They kissed, touched, caressed, and fondled like neither had done since Gulf Shores. They climbed slowly out of the infinity pool hand in hand, found a double chaise and collapsed into each other's arms where they fell asleep. This night was not about sex. Nor was it about sensuality. They knew they were overqualified on both accounts.

This was about two friends sharing each other. They caressed in their sleep—naked to the world just as they had been at the beach house. That's where they stayed for the night. No one would see. Tony was out for the evening. The cleaning crew would not return until Sunday. The landscapers wouldn't be back to mow until next Wednesday. This night belonged to them and them alone.

The sun creeped up in the morning, burning through the mist that rose from the river below. A farm next door afforded everyone within earshot ample opportunity to rise with the crowing rooster. Bridget and Mary Beth had barely moved in the night. But when the sunshine warmed their cheeks, they awoke as one. For a few minutes, they just lay there motionless, lost in each other's wanting eyes. Bridget moved first, stretching her hand out to pull Mary Beth closer and landing a kiss that was willingly—no, eagerly—returned.

Their caresses started to be more physical and the kissing more pronounced when the quiet was interrupted by a ping on MB's phone—one specifically assigned to Tony. It was not a welcome interruption, but she felt compelled to check.

It was from a burner phone that only she, Jack and Tony knew about.

"Will send message from other phone. Don't ask any questions. Don't say anything other than, 'Yes.'"

Mary Beth was confused; Bridget obviously had no clue what was going on. As they looked at each other in total bewilderment, the next text message pinged in.

"MB, will you marry me?"

Chapter 18—West end girl; redneck boy

Special Agent Rachel Whitney had not always been with the Federal Bureau of Investigation. Of course, no one is born into the crime-fighting unit, except perhaps J. Edgar Hoover. But Whitney actually had a career before the FBI—as a decorated officer with the Louisville Police Department.

Like Bridget and Mary Beth, Rachel was a Louisville native, but grew up in the city's west end instead of tony St. Matthews. There was no parochial school education for her. No, it was Coleridge-Taylor Elementary, Western Middle, and Central High. Her parents worked two jobs each to make sure their family was fed, clothed and housed in something better than the shotgun shanties they each had grown up in.

Marcus Whitney covered the late shift at Triangle Liquor on 23rd street most weekends, but his main job was as a pressman for the Louisville *Courier-Journal* where once he met Barry Bingham, the publisher and owner of the media empire that dominated the city. Bingham shook Marcus's hand on one chance meeting. It was like a celebrity encounter.

Rosalee Whitney rode the bus every day to a downtown hotel where she cleaned rooms and then crossed the street to wait tables at the Pendennis Club for the happy hour and dinner crowd that featured some of Louisville's society scions.

Brown v. Board of Education struck a blow to school segregation in 1954. No one bothered to tell Louisville that. The U.S. Supreme Court essentially ordered mandatory busing in the 1970s to reduce further school segregation. That news didn't make it to the West End either.

Rachel and her family dealt with it as best they could. She was a tremendous student graduating third in her class at Central High School — where she could have been valedictorian had it not been for the lecherous Mr. Miller who reduced her grade to a D in biology because she spurned his advances. It was then on to the University of Louisville for two years before she would transfer to Eastern Kentucky University to complete criminal justice studies.

It was at Eastern that she realized her vocation would, indeed, be law enforcement.

It was at U of L that she met Jack Adams.

Jack was a jock. Need more be said? He was captain of the second string, a chick magnet, confident beyond his years — thanks to Granddad — and ever on the prowl for a new conquest, which is one of the reasons why he spent as much time in the infirmary getting shots as he did on the playing field getting a shot at the NFL.

Theirs was a chance meeting — not at the football stadium, not at a fraternity rush party (Phi Alpha), nor at a social event at the student center. They met at the dumpster outside the campus grill where Rachel worked in the kitchen and Jack worked on his pick-up lines.

"He shoots; he scores," Jack boasted with his friends as he launched an empty drink container at the dumpster.

As the Dixie cup came to a rest short of the target, a voice to the side muttered, "Air ball!"

It was Rachel. Her kitchen whites were in stark contrast to her silky, mocha skin.

She picked up the errant cup and tossed it into the dumpster.

"Any more trash, or trash talk," she asked Jack and his cohorts.

Jack dismissed his cling-ons and approached the sweet, yet sassy adversary.

"I'm Jack Adams."

"I know who you are. And I'm the girl who cleans up your messes."

Jack was a little taken aback. Who was this guttersnipe to berate him? But she was cute. No, way beyond cute. Her hair was pulled back and hidden by a horrible net, but he could see the beauty that emanated from the whole person, not the headdress she wore.

Skin, mocha. Already established.

Eyes brown, but not the deep brown one would expect. These were light brown, almost tawny. So, too, was the hair crammed into the unflattering net that covered her head.

"You are beautiful. Did anyone ever tell you that?"

"And you are full of shit. Did anyone ever tell you that?

The initial encounter was but a fleeting memory for both Jack and Rachel when they started seeing each other on a regular basis away from the dumpster. They quickly became an item on campus because of his stature as a high-profile jock. He could basically have any girl he wanted; he chose the black girl from Louisville's west end. The gods were surely pulling a trick on the sorority sisters who longed only for their MRS degree.

They met in August. Started dating in a serious manner one week later. He spent more time with her than he did with the football team, a feat in and of itself. By October, he had fallen completely and totally in love. At the victory celebration after a win over East Tennessee, he asked her to marry him.

The world stopped spinning.

Two months into a relationship, and he was ready to tie the knot? Rachel obviously had powers she never dreamed of. But the feeling was quite mutual. Of course, she would have to finish her education and start a career; Jack would have to play out the string on whether football was in his long-term planning. But once the shock erased itself from her face…

"YES!"

Rachel was walking in rarified air. Jack was already in the stratosphere.

There are precious few examples of successful relationships being launched next to a dumpster, but theirs would be one.

They both knew it.

Both sets of parents had a different take on the situation.

Chapter 19 — Guess who's coming to dinner

It's about 225 miles from the west end of Louisville to Main Street in Pikeville, and also a light year or two in other regards. Jack made the trek frequently — not as frequently as his mother would like, but enough to keep Granddad sufficiently satisfied. Rachel had never been any further east than Shelbyville, a mere 20 miles from Louisville; her parents hadn't made it that far.

Clement Combs was different. Not only did he have houses scattered around the state and the country, he also traveled frequently in his private plane to locales outside the U.S.: fishing trips to the Caribbean, hunting trips to Canada, or sunning himself along with his companion on a Mexican beach while Mrs. Combs shopped on Fifth Avenue in New York. Jack's mother had traveled the world with her parents when she was younger, but was now content to stay in the friendly confines of Pike County where she watched a lot of television, ventured out only to stock up on groceries or visit Walmart, and cried a lot. Her physician had recommended Prozac; she chose Proverbs — Chapter 3, Verse 5. *Trust in the Lord with all your heart and lean not on your own understanding.*

It was only 225 miles, but worlds apart. Still, if Rachel and Jack were to move forward with wedding plans, the awkward meeting of families had to take place. But where? When? And is there an escape route?

They held off telling their families anything at all about their relationship until after Christmas. Why ruin the holidays by instigating a family feud that would rival the Hatfields and McCoys, which coincidentally started in Pike County. Wait until a more appropriate time — Valentine's Day. Who could be angry with a young couple in love on a day that celebrates romance?

Clement Combs could. Marcus and Rosalee Whitney both could and would.

The meeting took place in Frankfort so that neither family would be too inconvenienced. Granted, the state capital is much farther away from Pikeville than Louisville, but the Combs family was in Lexington for most of the UK basketball season.

It had to be in public so that neither patriarch would be tempted to raise his voice in an ungentlemanly manner.

Breaking bread is always good. Sitting down for supper in a busy restaurant would work. Rachel could tell her parents that she wanted to transfer to Kentucky State and asked them to visit the campus with her. Jack could convince Granddad to make the 30-minute trip from Lexington if for no other reason than just to see him.

The wheels were set in motion.

Saturday—D-Day. Nineteen hundred hours. Serafini's on Broadway. Reservations under Jack Adams *and* Rachel Whitney. The staff had been forewarned that the two reservations would be at the same table.

Clement arrived first with his wife and daughter--Jack's mother—close behind. They were seated at a table for eight.

"Young lady, I don't think this is right," Clement waved his arms at the empty chairs.

"This is the table reserved for Mr. Adams, sir. Let me check. In the meantime, may I get you something to drink?"

Clement ordered for everyone. Four Roses neat for him; Cabernet for his long-suffering wife; club soda for Jack's mother, who could not drink alcohol because of the antidepressant her doctor finally convinced her to try even though she preferred Ephesians over Effexor.

Children, obey your parents in the Lord, for this is right.

As the drinks were set before them, Marcus and Rosalee were brought to the table by the same hostess.

"Bethany will be right with you to get your drink orders. Enjoy."

The Whitney's were speechless. The Combs clan equally dumbfounded. Shortly after the Whitney's arrived, a complete and total stranger to both families strode in.

"I'm David Hensley, pastor at the Presbyterian Church here in Frankfort. I've been asked to join you tonight, but judging by the looks on your faces, I'm not sure why."

Jack and Rachel rounded the hostess station and caught sight of the mass confusion at the table they had reserved.

Rachel spoke first.

"Mom, dad, this is Jack."

"And this is Rachel."

In unison, they proclaimed to their families that "We're going to get married."

Applause erupted in the booths nearby. On cue, Bethany brought over a magnum of champagne.

There was no applause at their table. Marcus sat in disbelief; Clement stood in denial.

This would not end well.

At the conclusion of the evening, some two minutes later, Clement stormed out with his wife and daughter trailing close behind as they routinely did.

"Over my dead body." That is all he spoke. He slammed through the entry door and marched quickly to the Cadillac waiting for him and his entourage of two.

Rosalee never sat. She moved to Marcus and kneaded his tense shoulder muscles. He was not as quiet.

"Rachel, what in the name of all things holy are you thinking?"

He knew Jack from his football exploits. He knew Clement because he had seen his name on more than one occasion while he was running the presses at the *Courier*. The stories were never positive.

"You dare drag our good name down with this white trash?"

Whoa.

There was plenty of animosity to go around. The west end black family didn't like the rednecks from Pikeville and the feeling was quite mutual.

"I'm disappointed," Marcus's voice was low and shaky. "I'm more than disappointed, I'm devastated."

With that, he plunged his head into his hands as if hiding his eyes would make things better. Rosalee kept massaging his shoulders.

Pastor Hensley rose, turned to walk away, and left with a "Let me know what I can do to help. I'll be praying for you and your families."

Rosalee and Marcus also headed for the exit. Both looked at their daughter. Marcus cast a suspicious eye at Jack, but quickly returned his glare to Rachel. The door slammed behind them, helped in part by storm winds that were blowing through the ditch that is Frankfort.

Jack and Rachel collapsed into chairs around the empty table.

What the hell just happened, they wondered aloud?

Bubbly Bethany came back. "Would you like me to bring out the cake now?"

They had ordered a simple sheet cake from a nearby bakery. Plain cake, plain white icing. The only color was a Cardinal red monogram—RAJ for Rachel and Jack Adams.

"I don't think we'll be needing it," Jack said in a forlorn monotone. "You all enjoy it back in the kitchen."

"That went well." Rachel broke the silence with sarcasm dripping from her lips. "What are we going to do?"

"We're going to get married," Jack reassured her. "We're going to hold hands and say, 'I do.' We're going to make a life together forever."

The Montagues and Capulets established the baseline.

The Hatfields and McCoys brought it to new heights in Kentucky.

It may not be immortalized in literature lore, but the feud that was about to erupt between Clement Combs and Marcus Whitney would no doubt be monumental. The collateral damage would affect those they loved dearly, namely John Quincy Adams and Rachel Ann Whitney.

"We are going to be together forever," he said again trying to convince himself as much as he was trying to convince Rachel.

"I love you, Jack Adams!"

"And I love you, Rachel Whitney!"

They pulled each other together to share a kiss when Bethany returned.

"Here's your check. No rush. Hope you enjoyed your evening. Thank you for visiting Serafini's. Please come back soon."

She was expert in her delivery, albeit rote.

"Let me walk you to your car," Jack offered as any southern gentleman would do.

"It's across the way on Clinton."

They left the restaurant arm in arm. If they cut through the grounds of the Old Capitol, the trip would be quicker. Jack could see Rachel's old Ford Focus on the street. He also spotted an alcove behind the building that was hardly visible in three directions. The Focus could wait. His focus couldn't. They fell into each other's arms as soon as they hit the alcove.

The heavens immediately opened with a late winter rainstorm that bathed them, metaphorically washing away everything that had gone wrong that evening.

It was his first time in the secure confines of the Old Capitol. It would not be his last. Unfortunately, Rachel would not be a part of the future.

"We're going to be together forever," Jack repeated in his mind. He kissed his new fiancée goodnight and saw her off to Louisville. She would have to contend with her folks. He would have to contend with Granddad. At that exact moment, his phone rang. Clement. Should he answer? He was afraid not to.

"Hello?"

"Jack, it's your Granddad. Sorry I left in such a huff, but you really threw me—threw us all for a loop tonight.

"I'm not comfortable with what you propose, but I will keep an open mind. I only hope your negress's family can do the same."

MY WHAT?

Rachel a negress out of some Civil War era novel? Who are you, Clement, you old asshole? She will be my wife. This will be our life. Fuck you and fuck anyone who thinks like you. We're going to be married and we're going to be together forever.

It all sounded great in his head. He never breathed a single word.

"I'll talk with Rachel, Granddad. I know we can all get along as family."

"I'm sure you're right, Jack. No point in messing around with my will until we get this whole thing settled."

That was a gut punch and Clement knew it. As the only child of an only child, Jack stood to inherit millions from his grandfather. Clement was not about to take that off the table in his "negotiations" about Jack's future.

Marcus Whitney didn't have the financial leverage that Clement Combs did. But he did have the men's Bible study group at the Quinn Chapel AME church at his disposal, which included three retired police officers.

If Rachel insisted on entering a relationship with this redneck throw boy, she would do it with her eyes open to him, his family, and his friends—in Louisville and elsewhere.

The sound you hear now is the rattling of bones from the skeletons in Jack's closet. He was totally unaware; Rachel was totally unamused.

Chapter 20 — The South will never rise again

Kentucky was a border state during the Civil War. It sent native sons north and south in the War of Northern Aggression or the Great Southern Rebellion, depending on which side of the Mason-Dixon line your foot landed on. It wasn't until after the surrender at Appomattox that leaders in Kentucky determined that the state would side with the Confederacy — yes, the state backed losers in a game that had already been decided.

The trajectory was somewhat convoluted, but Marcus Whitney's family tree had roots that could be traced back through the lineage of noted horseman, Sonny Whitney, whose full name was Cornelius Vanderbilt Whitney. Yes, that Vanderbilt — the 19th Century rail tycoon and patron of the Nashville university that bears his name.

It really didn't matter. Marcus's great grandfather was a slave in Tennessee who adopted the surname of his master, an obscure distant relative of the noted philanthropist, and passed it on to his children, grandchildren, great grandchildren, and Rachel.

Jack Adams was on a different page of the ancestry.com website. The Adams part was a recent addition to Kentucky's gene pool, but Combs wasn't. It was the name of a former Governor, several judges, a handful of legislators, and countless political wannabes in city and county government. It was even the surname of a Louisville TV news reporter who went postal on her own family when her husband complained about her macaroni and cheese. She took out him, her son, and daughter before turning the gun on herself.

The Combs name was legend in the state. But it wasn't always in Clement's best interest — or as it turned out, in Jack's.

Shirley Combs, and why anyone would name a male child Shirley is still a mystery, was a survivor of the Battle at Perryville. He was part of the strategic retreat with General Braxton Bragg after the "rebels" had spanked the "yankees" in 1863.

Shirley continued his personal war against Northern Aggression until word reached him and his unit in the Florida Panhandle that General Lee had surrendered.

The devastated lieutenant started the long journey home to Eastern Kentucky where he and other likeminded Southern loyalists started their own chapter of the Ku Klux Klan, elements of which still exist in the state—elements, as it turns out, that are funded in part by generous corporate donations from Yellow Creek Energy.

Former Louisville Police Department Sergeant, Alan Stone found out all of that from a trip to the library, a phone call to the director of the Perryville Battlefield Museum, and a review of IRS tax forms on Guidestar. He was the first to report to Marcus at Bible study.

The second was a protégé of Marcus's father in the LPD, Lee Graeter. He had checked into Jack's social life on and off campus and came away, as no surprise to anyone, that Jack was a rounder. His co-ed exploits were the stuff of myth and legend—including an overnight stay with a Chi Omega *after* he had asked Rachel to marry him.

That alone would have been enough to send most women packing to get away from a cheating, racist fiancé. But that wasn't all—not by any stretch.

Jack was strictly second string behind Brett Miles at the QB position. Jack was just grateful for the opportunity to suit up as a "valuable member of the team," and more grateful for the bevy of beauties who liked quarterbacks regardless of where they ranked on the depth chart.

His position on the totem had not escaped the vigilant eyes of bookmakers, especially after game three when Miles went down with a knee injury. Jack was the man now! If he completed a pass to win the game, he would be the hero and subject to adoration across campus. If he struggled to find an open receiver, but went down to the onrush of defensive lineman, he would still be a hero.

Clement, of all people, sent an emissary to talk with Jack. Beat the spread here; don't cover the spread there. A lot of folks would be winners or losers depending on how Jack embraced the laces of a football. In other, simpler words, throw the game.

Dave Robinette brought that information to Marcus based on some confidential informants he maintained long after his retirement. They liked to dabble in off-track betting of the illegal variety. Robinette handed over the packet and warned, "You need to tell your daughter to stay away from this guy. He's trouble. No question about it, pure trouble."

If he cheated on his team, his school, and ignored his personal honor, would he cheat on her? Rachel didn't need to ask herself the question a second time. She knew.

It was the off-season right after spring practice. Jack was relaxing by the pool at his condo complex, thanks to Granddad, who referred to it as the Louisville office of Yellow Creek Energy, just as his accountant had told him.

A Jackie Collins romance novel was ostensibly his reading material to underscore the more sensitive and romantic side of the hard-body football player. Truth be known, Jack didn't know if the book was entertaining or even if it were upside down. He was peering, or more accurately leering over the pages of the book, yet behind the shelter of his Ray Bans at the buxom neighbors from 22B—right next door to his unit.

They took turns applying lotion or oil or cream or something to each other's bare backs while straps on their bikinis were undone. Jack really didn't care what they were applying, but did care about the entertainment value of it. Once the lube job was completed, both laid on the deck chaises face down, With the tops loosened, and the thongs covering, well covering practically nothing, there was not a lot left for an onlooker's imagination. Jack hadn't been involved in a threesome in quite a while. Perhaps his luck would change.

Oh, it did. For the worse, Much worse.

Rachel stormed through the gate, found her fiancé in mid-stare and tossed a weighty envelope toward his head. Before he had a chance to recover from the surprise attack, Rachel started a tirade that began with her voice low, but words pronounced very distinctly and with tremendous anger in her eyes.

"Deny it, asshole. Deny any part of it."

Perplexed, Jack removed a fistful of papers and started scanning the dossier that Marcus's prayer posse had compiled.

"Deny it Jack. Tell me that there is no truth to any of that crap."

As he raised his Ray Bans to his forehead, he looked at Rachel in total bewilderment. There is no metaphor, no idiom, nothing that could capture the severity of the moment adequately. No "cat that ate the canary," "hand in the cookie jar," "deer in the headlights." Nothing.

Their storybook romance was about to take a drastic and dark turn.

"Rachel, I…"

He never finished whatever lie he was getting ready to tell her.

"You son of a bitch. I was about ready to throw my life away with *you*! You can't deny it because it's all true, isn't it asshole?"

"Rach, we can fix this if you…"

"The only thing I want to fix right now, John Quincy Adams, is you."

For a fleeting moment, Jack thought that Rachel was sincere. That she would work with him to fix any problems and they could move on. That momentary loss of reality was quickly dispelled as Rachel continued.

"I would like nothing more than to convert you from a stud to a gelding. And if you come near me again, that is exactly what I'll do. Don't believe me? Try it."

With that, she stripped the engagement ring from her finger and threw it at Jack, who was still caught somewhere between bewilderment and anger.

"I won't be needing this anymore," her voice grew louder. "Maybe your Chi O will want it."

She stormed off as two carats of princess cut diamond bounced off Jack's shoulder and onto the pool deck.

"Rachel, wait!" He rose from the chair to follow her. She turned only long enough to flip him off. His efforts to reach her were interrupted as three burly figures moved between him and his fleeing fiancée. Alan Stone, Lee Graeter, and Dave Robinette. Then Marcus Whitney stepped in to complete the fearsome foursome.

"If you go near my baby again, I won't wait for her to cut your balls off; I'll do it myself. You got me QB?"

Silence.

"I said, you got me boy?" Marcus's voice was getting louder and more impatient. His three cohorts were starting to show that chilling stare that cops use to break weak lawbreakers.

"Yes, sir. I hear you."

Marcus turned to walk away when Jack added.

"I'm sorry, Mr. Whitney. Please tell Rachel I'm sorry. I had a great thing with her and I blew it. I wouldn't blame her if she never speaks to me again."

"Son, if she speaks to you — ever — I'll kick her ass as well as yours. This is over. Period."

Marcus and his posse turned to walk away. Jack retreated toward his chaise and scoured the deck for the ring.

"Here, Jack."

It was one of the young ladies from 22B.

"I saw what went on. I'm so sorry for you," her doe eyes were reeling Jack in like a Gulf mackerel. "If I can do anything to help, you just let me know."

Jack's brief pity party was over. Time to move on.

"Well, I am grilling a nice piece of salmon tonight if you and your roommate would like to come over. I could use the company."

In the parking lot, Rachel put her car in gear, tore off onto Brownsboro Road and back toward downtown. Tears filled her eyes making it all the more difficult to navigate rush hour traffic. This was her wake up call. Follow your heart, but make sure your head is in the game. Her heart had said 'yes,' perhaps too early. But her head was never consulted. Thankfully, her father and his friends had done the work for her. Never again. Never again would she be played by someone like Jack Adams. A pledge to herself.

And as for Jack, the KKK descendent and his sugar-daddy, racist grandfather; Jack, the lying and cheating boy wonder of U of L. Jack, the Pike County piece of shit; Jack would be erased from her life forever! Or, until D.C. called.

Chapter 21 — Welcome home

Following the split with Jack, Rachel threw herself into her studies. The plan all along was two years at U of L and then finish at EKU in criminal justice. She was a first-round draft pick in the law enforcement lottery. She graduated at the head of her class; passed every assessment exam ever given her with flying colors; and, with apologies to affirmative action, she was black, and she was a she.

Offers poured in from around the country from virtually every police department coast to coast — metropolitan or Mayberry.

She settled on Louisville. The return home was good for her. It allowed her to be in a community she loved and wanted to 'protect and serve.' It also afforded her an opportunity to be closer to her parents, who both had fallen on hard times medically. Marcus had developed lung cancer despite the fact that he had never smoked; Rosalee suffered from early onset dementia, which meant she could do little to care for her husband.

Rachel worked 24-7, or at least it seemed like it. Daytime, it was catching the bad guys; at night, she traded her gold shield for a red cross and became Clara Barton for her folks. That part of her job, unfortunately, didn't last long.

Marcus died three months after she moved back to Louisville.

Rosalee only six weeks after Marcus. The cruelty of dementia tested her daily on the simplest of questions like what she had eaten for breakfast. But her heart knew something was missing — Marcus. She could not have that; she could not stand being without him. It's almost as if she willed herself to follow on whatever journey God had in store for them.

Rachel was inconsolable. In the span of just a few weeks, she had lost both her mother and her father. She was over Jack, but that pain had left a scar that would never go away. She needed a change—something that wouldn't eliminate her pain, but that could certainly ease it. A new town; a new set of work colleagues; new friends she hadn't even met. But get the hell out of Louisville.

The FBI would be her ticket out; the FBI would be her ticket back.

Rachel negotiated with her captain to get a favorable recommendation on her FBI application. He had no reservations about her abilities. Quite the contrary. He didn't want to lose her.

The application moved through the approval process much the same as prey moves through a python—*Slowly*.

Once accepted, however, everything moved at warp speed.

Quantico for the Academy. Passed with flying colors.

San Juan for the first assignment. Drug connection exposed in large part because of her undercover work.

Los Angeles. Bank robbers who fashioned themselves after some Bonnie and Clyde fixation.

Atlanta. Joint task force with Homeland Security to bring down an ISIS cell in Buckhead.

Charlotte. Nothing yet, but she had only been there a few days. She was just figuring out where the restrooms were when she got a call.

"Agent Whitney," a stern voice sounded on the other end of the phone. "District Director O'Brien. We have a special assignment for you. Are you interested?"

"With all due respect, sir, where and what?"

"Kentucky. Working out of the Louisville office, but investigating in Frankfort. We've been hearing some chatter from CI's about legislative vote buying. And…"

His pause was long enough to be uncomfortable.

"And what, sir?"

"And one of the targets of the investigation is Jack Adams. I believe you know him?"

Know him. Loathe him. What is that redneck rascal up to now?

"Sir, I'm sure you have had someone look into the history that Jack and I have."

"We have."

"And you still want me on the case?"

"We do, Agent Whitney. You know the state; you know the background of at least one of our targets; you know more about what's going in Kentucky than anyone else in the agency."

"Sir, I hope you know that if I take this assignment, I will not let my past interfere with what can and should be done as it relates to Mr. Adams."

"Rachel, if I weren't sure of that, we wouldn't be on this call.

"So, I'll take that as a yes. Your field agent in charge will be Walker Gross. He's in Louisville. Get the next plane out of Charlotte and report to Gross no later than day after tomorrow. His team, will bring you up to speed, but *you* will control the mission. Call me anytime—day or night—if you have questions or problems. This is my personal cell number—202-555-1863. Use it as you need to."

"Yes, sir."

"Whitney, this is an important investigation. Political corruption is rampant in the U.S. Kentucky is at or near the top of the list. Always has been. I worked BOPTROT years ago. It hasn't gotten any better since then, only more sophisticated."

"I understand, sir."

"Rachel," his voice suddenly less authoritarian. "I know this is your home. I know the history you have with Jack Adams, I would never want to put you in a position that would compromise you and your beliefs. Please tell me whether we're good to go on this."

"Sir, we are good. My history with Jack is just that—history. I told him once before that if he crossed me, I'd cut off his balls. If what you say is true, he has crossed me professionally. Need I say more?"

On the plane ride from Charlotte to Louisville, Rachel read the transcript of conversations recorded among legislators, Big Tony, Mary Beth, and Jack. Yes, Jack. Tears welled in the corners of her eyes. This is not what she had pictured. Not what she had imagined. Not what Jack had promised her.

That was then. This is now.

Jack Adams, you have the right to remain silent…

As she mirandized him in her thoughts, a glimmer of hope was unwavering. That was until she and Walker Gross met to discuss where the investigation stood and the status of those being targeted.

She thought to herself, "You, Jack Adams, are toast. And so are your friends. Paybacks are hell, aren't they?"

Chapter 22—Can you be a carpetbagger from the South?

Tamara Looney was everything Stuart Carroll wasn't. Confident, poised, eloquent, elegant, and attractive. She was Katrina Van Tassel to his Ichabod Crane. There was nothing romantic, of course. Stuart had no time for affairs of the heart, even though at 44, Tamara could still turn heads in the halls of the capitol. No, Stuart was more enamored with her power. She exuded it, and she earned the right to do so.

Decorated war veteran from one of those 'shock and awe' moments in the Middle East.

Tops in her class at Emory University undergrad and law school.

Clerked for a powerful U.S. Circuit Court Judge in Atlanta.

Youngest person to be nominated as an Assistant U.S. Attorney.

Frequently mentioned as a candidate for Georgia's Attorney General.

From her Shirley Temple curls, which she refused to straighten, to the dimples when she smiled, she was going to be a great television candidate—a rising star in Georgia politics. That all came to a screeching halt when her husband was offered a position as chief of thoracic surgery at the University of Louisville College of Medicine.

She was the media darling who got headlines, conducted the news conferences, and traveled in circles that included judges, managing partners from Atlanta's largest law firms, and the politically powerful, including the Governor.

Dave Tunie, her husband of six years, was brilliant, shy, unassuming, adept at microsurgery procedures, and a rising star himself in the medical universe.

Dave was a carpetbagger from Michigan who rode his talent and IQ to a full scholarship at Emory. That's where he met Tamara — blind date set up by one of his fraternity brothers and a close friend of hers from Macon, where she grew up. After hearing about Dave from her friend, her expectations were low. After meeting him, they were even lower.

Yet there was something about him that drew her in — certainly not his looks, he was an intellectual equal but not superior, and he was content to stand in a corner and watch her work a room rather than hang by her side and make awkward attempts at conversation. It wasn't love at first sight, but it was mutual intrigue from the outset.

Tamara set the tone of the relationship. She actually had to call him for a second date and following a two-year courtship, she tired of waiting on him, and finally proposed herself. She was deeply in love, and those around her could never figure out why. It was probably the same clumsy characteristics that made her like Stuart so much.

Yes, they made the move to Louisville — at her insistence. Her rationale was that she could be a great prosecutor no matter where she practiced. The bad guys would always be there. Dave might never get another opportunity like this, or at least not this early in his career. And there was that little matter of a phone call from Governor Aaron Miller. Miller was a friend of Damien Lyons, who had confided that he was going to run for Governor of Kentucky in three years. Political discussions in the Bluegrass State are sort of like 'Law and Order' reruns. You don't have to wait long for another to come along.

In his conversation with his mentor, Lyons confided that he had a weakness, well two (that he admitted to). One was gender. The man, now on this fourth wife, carried little fascination with women voters who, according to polling, found him to be smug, condescending, and borderline sexist, which reinforces what good polling can tell you. His other weakness was in Louisville where he lost to a mythical candidate in almost every matchup. Apparently, when you take public swipes at a popular former mayor, and a popular sitting Congressman, people remember.

Miller had the answer. He always did ever since they spent eight years together in a Tennessee boarding school. "Let me make a call. This could work well for you, Damien."

Tamara Looney was accustomed to getting calls from powerful people who wanted to curry favor with the U.S. Attorney's office. You can figure out why. She had never been called, though, by a sitting Governor—her Governor.

"Tamara, it's Aaron."

"Excuse me?"

"Aaron Miller—you know the guy who sits in that stuffy old office in the capitol."

She snapped to attention as she would have done had a superior officer approached her during her Army career.

"Sir, I'm sorry. I didn't recognize..."

"Don't worry about it," he interrupted. "And don't call me Sir. It's Aaron."

"Yes sir, I mean Aaron. To what do I owe this pleasure?"

"I don't trust telephones," he laughed. "You never know when your office will have the FBI listening in."

She managed a weak chuckle.

"Meet me at the coffee shop in Buckhead, across from the mall. Say tomorrow morning at 7:30. Work for you?

"I'll make it work, sir. I mean Aaron. I mean Governor. Sir, I don't know what I mean."

The unflappable Tamara Looney had just become unglued.

"I'll explain more tomorrow," Miller said. "Just be ready to pack your bags."

She didn't sleep that night. It was the first of many sleepless nights to come.

At the coffee shop, she took a table in the back corner, which his state trooper detail had cleared, right after they swept the place for listening devices and formed a human wall around the table to prevent curious patrons from firing up their smartphones for pictures, recordings, or videos.

She came to attention when Miller nudged through the wall of police. They shook hands, he motioned her to sit, and sent one of the troopers for coffee. Nothing fancy for either. Large, regular coffee. Hold the mocha, caramel, strawberries and cream, pumpkin spice, and pretension.

"I hear Dave has been offered a job in Kentucky."

He heard? How did he hear? Her mother didn't even know yet.

"Yes sir, he has been. We're wrestling with a decision."

"First of all, I told you yesterday not to call me sir. I'm Aaron. You're Tamara. We're friends."

Sometime in the next few minutes, he would also use the word 'buddy,' but she didn't know that it was a synonym for political bullshit.

"If you say so," the word slipped from her lips. "Aaron."

"Better. Here's a little friendly advice, tell him to take it. Pack your bags, sell your house, and be on the next plane out of here."

She was dumbfounded. Was the Governor really ordering her to leave the state? Was it a mere suggestion, or a mandate?

"Let me explain," he started.

"Please do," was her catatonic response.

"You are a great public servant, Tamara. You're in this business for all of the right reasons. From a political standpoint, you can stay here and be a mid-sized fish in a great big pond, or you can go to Kentucky where you will become a big fish in a little bitty pond."

"I'm afraid I have no idea what you're talking about."

Miller continued, "It's like this. You can stay here in the U.S. Attorney's office busting the bad guys, grabbing a few headlines because of terrorist cell arrests, and trying to establish a political base to run against families that have generations of money and might. But bottom line, honey, is you're going to be handicapped by your lack of political pedigree and your redneck roots."

Tamara bristled a little at the Governor's frankness, and the fact that he called her honey. True, her political pedigree only included a two-year stint by her grandfather as an interim mayor after the elected mayor of Macon was arrested on fraud charges. And 'redneck roots' was accurate, although just about anyone outside the Atlanta metro area could be labeled as such. In fact, some wore it as a badge of honor.

"I don't mean to offend you, Tamara. I just want to be honest with you because I see the potential that you have, and I want to support it as you develop your political acumen.

"Damien Lyons in Kentucky is a buddy of mine. We have been friends since serving time together at the McCallie School in Chattanooga. He has confided in me that he is putting the infrastructure in place to run for Governor."

And this means what to Dave and me, she thought.

"The election is not for three years. Plenty of time for you to move, attach yourself to the U.S. Attorney's office and prosecute some high-profile cases — especially those that are drug related or that crack down on white collar criminals, both of which poll well for a "tough on crime" candidate. The federal government can stamp your ticket while you're building a base and a following among voters — especially with women, and especially in Louisville where Dave will be practicing. If I say so, Damien will add you to his ticket as Lieutenant Governor."

"And why would he do that," she asked innocently.

"Because he wants to be Governor and I can help him, but he knows that support will be more committed if he listens to me on the running mate issue. I know you can do the job, and after you spend time in Frankfort, I will support you in a run for the Senate just like I'm going to do when my term is up; we'll be colleagues in D.C. in a few years."

He had her life all planned. At this point, she didn't know which end was up, and Miller was already picking out window treatments for her new townhouse in Arlington.

"Let me have some time," she asked with the look of bewilderment growing more pronounced.

"I understand, Tamara, but make it quick. I hear Dave needs to have an answer by the fifteenth. That's less than two weeks away."

He heard? How did he… She discontinued her own thoughts and moved on to the challenge and opportunity Miller had outlined.

After coffee with the Governor, she continued her day at the office. Not a busy time. No court dates for three weeks. Research staff, paralegals, and FBI agents bordered on frantic, Tamara did not.

She allowed her daydreaming to drift to Zillow and Google searches about Louisville. Nice houses. Less expensive than Atlanta. Nice city. U of L hospital was top notch. U.S. Attorney was a new presidential appointee, and they did share Order of the Coif status.

Louisville would get Dave closer to his family in Ann Arbor, and still be relatively close to her family in Macon. They didn't have children to uproot and move to a new school. Their Morkie was pretty flexible about where she took her next meal.

Lieutenant Governor Looney? Had a nice ring to it.

On her way home that night, she stopped at Marshall's Liquor about three blocks from her house. After she arrived at home, she took a quick shower, donned her sexiest negligee, turned the lights down low, put a little Toni Braxton on the sound system, and waited for Dave to come home.

"Are we celebrating something," he asked in the best non-geek voice he could muster. Coat off, briefcase down, tie loosened. He moved toward his stunning wife.

"Here," she cooed as she handed him a glass with an amber liquid over ice.

"What is this," he asked still trying to maintain non-geek status.

"Woodford Reserve," she said as she approached him with no reservations at all.

"Bourbon? You hate bourbon."

"Not any more. It's produced in our New Kentucky Home."

"You mean?"

"Yes, we're on the move."

With that, she slowly poured her glass of elixir down from her neck, over her breasts, past her stomach and onto her thighs.

"Baby, I have just created your own Bourbon Trail!"

He was a geek, but he wasn't an idiot. He started tasting the bourbon on her neck and followed it all the way to her thighs — plural.

Big fish. Little pond. Yes, indeed, she liked those odds.

Chapter 23 — Here comes the bride

Mary Beth and Bridget looked at each other in disbelief. Then at the phone, and back to each other.

'MB, will you marry me?'

Mary Beth knew that something was wrong; terribly wrong. She and Tony had a wonderful relationship, but more akin to brother and sister than husband and wife. He had to be doing this for a reason, the rationale of which escaped her, but she knew he would explain when they were together.

"What are you going to do," Bridget asked still in a complete state of bewilderment.

"This changes nothing with us," Mary Beth said trying to reassure herself as much as she was Bridget. "I know Tony has his reasons. It's a pretty drastic ask, but I'm sure he knows what he's doing."

At least she hoped he did. So, too, did Bridget. She started typing — all caps.

'OH TONY! YES! YES! (heart emoji) (ring emoji) U HAVE MADE ME SO HAPPY (bride emoji)'

She looked at Bridget with eyes that asked for permission to hit the "send" button. Bridget nodded. MB tapped her phone and the text message was on its way. Was she about to become Mrs. Tony Barrows?

They waited anxiously now holding onto each other's hand. The phone pinged with an incoming message.

'U have made me the happiest man on the planet. We celebrate tonight! See you at home, and bring Bridget. She will want to share in the festivities.'

What the hell did that mean? The puzzlement was cut short with another ping.

'And we also need to clean the place. Company's coming.'

Company? Who? Why clean? What the hell was he talking about? Tony's first use of code. More—much more—would follow.

'Explain when I see you. Love you!'

'Love you 2 (lips emoji). See you at home.'

They were still lying next to each other as they had throughout the night. The sun was getting warmer raising tiny beads of sweat on their naked bodies, but the passion they had shared mere moments ago was lost—hopefully not forever. Now, though, was a time to take stock in what just happened, what it meant, and what the future held for them. Only Tony could tell them and, best case scenario, he wouldn't be home for 15 minutes.

They busied themselves getting ready for his arrival. A hot shower—separately. No time for extracurriculars. They dressed comfortably in running shorts and tank tops. Bridget called her boss to explain that there had been a family emergency and she would not be able to make the 9:00. As she cradled the phone between her ear and shoulder, she poured a generous amount of Pure Blue vodka over ice in two glasses. Mary Beth, who was trying to whip up a little breakfast, reached into the fridge and handed Bridget some OJ. This day would go a lot easier with a stiff drink—starting now.

They sat cross-legged next to each other on one of the Chesterfields munching on bacon and toast, washing it down with their screwdrivers.

Fifteen minutes had passed; it seemed like fifteen hours. Tony was late, which only added to their anxiety.

The door finally flew open and Tony burst in.

"MB, honey! I am the happiest man alive!"

He stared at the two addled and confused women in front of him.

"You started without me," as he raised one of their glasses and took a sip. "Bridget, I'll have what you're having. Mary Beth, let's dance. Put on some music and let's get this engagement thing officially started."

They weren't Stepford Wives, but they moved almost as mechanically and methodically—still with no clue as to what was happening.

With the music blaring the sound of the Temptations doing 'My Girl,' Tony started slow dancing with Mary Beth. He kissed her gently on the top of her head, then bent to kiss her cheek, at which time he whispered:

"We are being watched. Don't know why, don't know who, but we are being watched. They may even be listening. Smile."

He spun her around, she beamed, and he pulled her close again.

"Let's assume the worse. It's the law and they're after me for whatever reason. If we are married, they can't make you testify against me. I don't know where this is headed, but we need a good defense. That's the best I could think of."

"Company's coming," she repeated the words from his text.

"Search warrant will be issued tomorrow by Judge Lee. Friend of mine. Clerk gave me the heads up. Frankfort PD, but could go higher. No idea what they're looking for until I see the warrant."

He dipped her slightly, pulled her up and spun her around gently.

"And Bridget? Share in the festivities?"

"If we need to move anything out of here, it can't be me and it can't be you. Cops know us too well. She's new in town. No time to get involved with us. She can be our escape route if you think she is willing. Is she?"

Mary Beth moved her head to the side to peak around Tony's shoulder. There was Bridget leaning against the kitchen island. This is not the reunion Mary Beth had hoped for, but she was thankful that Bridget hadn't already headed for the door.

Mary Beth would do anything to help Tony.

Would Bridget do anything to help her?

Chapter 24 — I do, I think

Many years ago, young lovers in the Bluegrass State — especially Central and Southern Kentucky — would elope to Jellico, Tennessee, a heartbeat away from the state line. It was easy: no waiting period, no blood test, and no questions. Little wedding chapels popped up in Jellico, then along I-75 as the interstate system was developed, all the way to Gatlinburg and Pigeon Forge--or redneck Disneyland. Kentucky saw revenue leaving the state, and decided to get competitive — a blessing for Tony and Mary Beth.

They could get a marriage license in the morning, see a magistrate in the afternoon, and celebrate their honeymoon in evening without ever having to leave Frankfort. Tony had already checked that out. And the magistrate would be able to work him in regardless of scheduling conflicts because he was one of the old customers from the paper route who had a dachshund that went missing before Tony found 'Klaus' and returned him.

As the music changed from the Temps to the Tops and 'Same Old Song,' Tony motioned MB and Bridget toward the basement and into his wine cellar to get something "old and expensive to liven up this party."

The wine room was solid concrete walls with a veneer of rugged brick salvaged from an old distillery that had been razed. More than 100 bottles neatly stacked in racks around the room caused sound echoes as voices bounced off the glass in the cavern.

"If they can hear us in here, we deserve to be caught."

Tony's confidence did little to comfort Mary Beth and Bridget.

"Here's what I know. Judge Lee is going to sign a warrant tomorrow requested by the Frankfort Police Department to search the house. That I know. What I don't know is what they're looking for or why they're coming in. I can only assume it has something to do with this."

He reached into his jacket pocket and produced a photo of Governor Damien Lyons, among others, at a 1 PP soiree.

"This was with the PD's request for the warrant."

MB and Bridget repeated the engagement cadence: look at each other, look at the picture, look back at each other.

"I have a call into my guys in the department to find out what they know. I think it's a fishing expedition, but you can never tell. There also is a rumor that the FBI is in town…"

Those three letters sparked a new level of concern for Mary Beth and her friend.

"But I'm not really sure about that, yet. There have been rumors of the FBI being in town every year since BOPTROT and nothing else has ever happened," Tony whistled past the graveyard.

"We need to be smart. I'll get a look at the warrant late this afternoon or first thing in the morning. My guy who clerks for Judge Lee will scan it and send it over. Once we see what it is they're trying to root out, we can take whatever steps necessary to make sure they come up dry."

Bridget finally broke into Tony's soliloquy, "And this affects me how?"

She was the new kid in town. First full day in the cesspool that is Frankfort politics — and only because she longed for her friend and lover, Mary Beth. Why was she being drawn into this game of sheriff cat and criminal mouse?

"Bridget, I can explain it all later," implored Mary Beth with a tremble in her voice and in her hand as she reached to take Bridget's. "I know it has been a long time since we were together, but I never forgot you as, first and foremost, my friend. I need you now. I need you to have my back for a few days. I'll make it up to you someday, somehow, but please say 'Yes.'"

A long silence followed MB's impassioned plea. The silence was broken by a string of sounds that only complicated matters further.

The intercom in the wine cellar buzzed from the entry gate.

"Dammit, Tony. I forgot the friggin' code," screamed a nearly incoherent Jack Adams either a) hungover, b) already on his way to a mid-morning buzz, or c) looking for bourbon to go along with the coke he had recently enjoyed.

Next in line in the assault on eardrums was Tony's phone and a ringtone from the old Dragnet TV show.

Dum-da-dum-dum.

"Whatta you got?"

Silence as Tony listened to the caller, a detective with FPD.

"Are you sure?"

More silence.

"Okay. Give me at least 30 minutes notice before you all swoop in tomorrow."

Tony collapsed into one of the leather gooseneck chairs in the wine cellar where his sommelier would instruct him on the attributes of a true connoisseur. The leather was cool. He could feel the chill through his clothes. It calmed him—but only momentarily.

Mary Beth had saved Jack from his solitary confinement at the gate, and led the bleary-eyed playboy to the basement. Bridget had been alone with Tony in the wine cellar. She didn't know him well at all, but she could see something was changing in his demeanor—visibly changing. His eyes grew wild, his skin flushed, his breathing heavy, but short. At the exact moment when Jack and Mary Beth came in, Tony's transformation from David Banner to the Incredible Hulk was complete.

He pushed his large frame out of the chair, knocking it back into a shelf of Pinot Grigio. Fortunately, nothing broke—a short-lived miracle. He flailed his arms wildly, taking with him several varieties of Cabernet with his left and an equal number of ports with his right.

"It's that little fucking weasel, Stuart Carroll," he bellowed like a wounded animal. "He's responsible for the picture, he's the one who got the police involved, he's the son-of-a-bitch trying to put us in jail."

Mary Beth and Bridget clung to each other more concerned than afraid. Jack settled into one of the chairs that remained upright, and pretended to be outraged while he searched his pockets for the balance of his blow.

"I'm going to kill the little fucker. I told him I would if he ever came after me. The asshole is dead. DEAD."

He pounded the table with both fists, not once but three times before Mary Beth approached him as someone would a strange dog. Hand extended. Eyes fixed. Calm breathing. No words. Tony started to relax; his angry rush of adrenaline retreating by the second. His breathing more sedate. He eyes less inflamed. She exuded a comforting aura and he was receptive to it.

When she finally grasped his hand and pulled herself closer to him, she stood on her tiptoes and whispered, "Stuart later. Right now, we have to plan a wedding."

She pulled back and smiled.

It was only after MB and Tony had played out their beauty and the beast routine, that Bridget finally answered Mary Beth.

"Yes, Mary Beth. I'll have your back — forever."

The Chambers Brothers took over the sound system as the four made their way from the wine cellar to the deck overlooking the river.

Now the time has come (Time)

There is no place to run (Time)

I might get burned up by the sun (Time)

But I had my fun (Time)

I've been loved and put aside (Time)

I've been crushed by tumbling tide (Time)

Chapter 25 — Bells will be ringing; birds will be singing

Most people have heard of the "six degrees of separation." It's the parlor game where anyone can trace themselves through six or fewer steps to virtually anyone else living, or in some cases, departed. For example, Big Tony's mother came to Kentucky from Philadelphia. Her parents were first-generation immigrants from Naples. Her father was a post-World War II worker whose job was to restore order and civility in the region. He was asked to help by a family friend named Leonardo Allegretti. Allegretti was Benito Mussolini's *aide de camp* who dodged a war crimes trial by assisting Allied forces once Mussolini had been banished to Northern Italy.

Long and short of it is that Tony was six degrees away from Mussolini.

But this is Kentucky. In most cases, there are only three degrees of separation required to make a connection.

The next morning, Tony was roused from a deep, and wine-induced sleep by a text from his friend in the judge's office that said a copy of the search warrant had been emailed to him. He stumbled to a desk in his room and opened his laptop. Better to read it on a larger screen than on his phone—especially given how bleary his eyes were.

'Blah...blah...blah...any and all electronic and/or hard copy files related to any member of the legislature and their staffs, any member of the executive branch and their staff members, and any lobbyist, lobbying firms, or companies registered with the Legislative and/or Executive Ethics commissions.'

"Fishing," he screamed loud enough to wake everyone else in the house, or wake the dead.

"The little fuck is doing nothing but leading a fishing expedition. Do they think I'm fucking stupid?"

The roar from the master bedroom reverberated throughout 1 PP. Even as MB, Jack and Bridget tried to return to sleepy-town, it was futile. All three eventually made their way to the kitchen where Tony had already started a pot of coffee. Mary Beth was half-asleep but did manage to get scrambled eggs going on the range. Speaking of scrambled, Jack's cocaine hangover had his brain shaken, not stirred. A little "hair of the dog" is what he needed to calm his nerves, as he quietly made his way, ironically, to the powder room for a quick snort. Bridget curled up on one of the Chesterfields and waited for the next shoe to drop.

Tony fired the first salvo in a barrage of strategy statements to come.

"Stuart Carroll must think I'm the dumbest asshole on this or any other planet.

"Does he really think I'm stupid enough to leave this shit lying around?

"You all know me better than that. Well, Bridget, we just met, but Jack and MB, you know.

"I think we have a little fun with the prick. I'm going to rename all of my old basketball tourney videos with the names of key legislators and members of the cabinet. Can you imagine how pissed they're going to be when they open the Damien Lyons file and find video of the UK-Duke game in '78?"

Mary Beth listened while she was serving up the eggs and toast. Jack listened, or about half-way listened as he returned from the powder room. Bridget listened more intently than anyone because she could sense that something was coming for her; something that made her a little uneasy.

Tony moved to a wall safe hidden behind Mary Beth's version of Rockwell's "Chain of Gossip" that featured some of her colleagues from LRC. He leaned his large frame over the safe to conceal the keypad and punched in the code. He reached his bear paw into the safe and extracted a thumb drive, dwarfed in his giant right hand.

"Bridget, I need you to hold onto this. It has a copy of every audio and video recording we have in support of the right to work bullshit. Names, dates, expectations, commitments. It all lives right here on this little bitty drive. You're new to our family. They won't suspect you."

Bridget looked at Mary Beth hoping to see some sign of assurance. Mary Beth nodded, so Bridget took the drive and crammed it into the running shorts that had served as her pajamas for the previous night.

"OK, then," said an excited Tony. "Let's get this wedding thing started!"

Jack was confused but agreed to be best man. Bridget was comforted that her role wouldn't be any more involved. Tony suggested someone other than she serve as the maid of honor because she had responsibilities assigned to her other than MOH. MB offered the name of her LRC mentor and mother *in absentia*, Jane Hupman.

Tony, Mary Beth, and Jack drove into town to get the marriage license. They grabbed a quick bite at Seraphini's where Jack washed down his Hot Brown with three fingers of Wild Turkey.

At 1:50, they met Jane at the courthouse. The magistrate, Dickie Gilliam, looked over the paperwork, asked if everyone was there of their own accord, and proceeded with the civil ceremony. In the background, they could hear the local church bells competing with each other for attention at 2:00.

By 2:15, Tony and Mary Beth were husband and wife. Jane was giddy with excitement for her protégé. Jack was off to the men's room for a leak and a lift as the coke spoon reappeared.

They were all back at 1 PP by 2:45 — all except Jane who returned to the Annex for work, and Bridget, who left earlier insisting that she had to check in with her boss before he thought she was MIA.

The cork from the Korbel almost broke a lamp as Tony and Mary Beth started celebrating their newly wedded bliss. Jack had accompanied them back to the river house, but decided to leave before the police showed up with their warrant, which could trap him in a drug dragnet he didn't want or need.

Jack's Jaguar had barely cleared the driveway when the police approached the gate. Sergeant Brent Cyrus slammed his hand on the intercom button.

"This is the Frankfort Police Department. We have a warrant to search the premises."

Tony buzzed the gate open and moved to the front porch to welcome his unwelcomed guests.

"Come in, ladies and gentlemen," he said as six police officers climbed out of their squad cars and moved toward the house. Cyrus barked out orders on which officers were to go to which floors as he presented Tony a copy of the warrant—a copy that he had seen earlier that morning.

"You'll have to excuse the mess. Mary Beth and I were just married, and we have been celebrating a bit."

Cyrus and the others ignored the warning and goose-stepped into the house. Two officers went upstairs, two went to the basement, and two—including Sergeant Cyrus—stayed on the main floor.

Fifteen minutes. Thirty minutes. Forty-five minutes passed. The police searched frantically; Tony and Mary Beth sat calmly.

As the police reconvened in the kitchen area, Tony broke the tension proclaiming that "It's five-o'clock somewhere. Care to join us?"

With that, he poured himself and his new bride a Maker's and soda. Cyrus declined on behalf of his officers.

"Mr. Barrows, we are seizing property as a result of this search that will be turned over to detectives in the FPD for review and evaluation. Do you understand?"

He held out three discs, but no paper copies of anything.

"Sergeant, I do, and I regret that you'll not only see UK's win over Duke in '78, but you will also see the heartbreaking loss against Christian Laettner and Duke in '92. I do wish you would stay to join us in toasting our marriage."

Cyrus was addled, not just confused. He declined again on behalf of his officers and marched to the door.

As they climbed into their cruisers, Tony had one last parting shot, "And wait until you see what UK did against Shaq and LSU in 1990!"

He slammed the door hard as the cruisers turned back toward the highway.

"Stuart Carroll is a dead man."

"Tony, calm down a little. We're good right now. Let's keep our heads down until the time is right. I don't want to be a widow on day one!"

Tony managed a weak smile and gave Mary Beth a kiss on top of her head.

"Honestly, MB, I don't know what I'd do without you."

Thirty miles west of 1 PP, Special Agent Walker Gross was at a Shelbyville hotel wearing out the carpet as he paced in a secure meeting room. Secure, he knew, because his colleagues had swept it and stood sentry outside the room and the hotel itself.

A few minutes before 5:00, Rachel Whitney entered the room and exchanged pleasantries with Gross. This was her show. She was the director. He was merely the producer providing the necessary support with other FBI agents.

Promptly at 5:00, two guests were escorted into the meeting room. Tamara Looney and Stuart Carroll—brought separately to the site by agents whose only words to them had been, "FBI, please come with me."

Looney was curious. Carroll was terrified. Rachel Whitney spoke first.

"Thank you for agreeing to join us," though agreeing was a bit of a stretch. "I'm Special Agent Rachel Whitney with the Federal Bureau of Investigation. This is my colleague, Special Agent Walker Gross."

Looney grew more curious; Carroll more terrified.

"What we say here is in complete confidence, but I am sure you both are willing to assist with our investigation. Otherwise, we wouldn't have invited you."

'Invited' may be an overreach, but the two continued to listen to Agent Whitney.

"We have launched an investigation into a vote-buying scheme that involves public officials and other political figures who are familiar to you both. What we're asking for is your cooperation in furthering our investigation."

Dumb stares from the Lieutenant Governor and the journalist.

"We know that there is an underbelly in our society bent on taking down our institutions and we want to do everything we can to stop it."

Tamara Looney raised her eyes to look more intently at the speaker, Agent Whitney. Now she remembered what had been plaguing her since she walked into the room. Those are the same words the agent had used in Atlanta to bring down an ISIS terrorist cell. She hadn't recognized the name because Whitney had been undercover; nor did she recognize the face because it was made up to look so unlike the natural beauty that was Rachel.

"I know you!"

"Yes, governor, and I know you. It's good to see you again."

Stuart interrupted as only a geek of his stature could.

"Well, I don't know you. I don't know why I'm here. And I demand to be released."

Rachel turned her head and glared at Stuart.

Tamara intervened on her behalf with a simple statement.

"Stuart, sit down and shut up."

Rachel continued.

"I can't emphasize enough the confidential nature of our discussion. We know that there are certain elements in Frankfort that are attempting to exchange money for favorable votes on legislation in the upcoming session.

"At the same time, Mr. Carroll, we know that you have been involved in your own amateur investigation..."

"AMATUER," Stuart protested.

"Mr. Carroll, if it weren't amateurish, why did we find it so easy to discover you?"

Stuart pushed himself from the air of indignation at the front of his chair to the 'Okay, I'll shut up' resignation at the back part of the chair.

"Agent Whitney," asked Tamara, "what are we supposed to do?" "First, Mr. Carroll, you will continue your personal investigation into lobbying and lobbyists as it relates to illegal activities to influence votes. We can't offer you any 'confirm or deny,' but we will not stand in the way of whatever arrangement you have with the FPD. In exchange, you will report to us any new findings you unearth on your own and as a result, will be given an exclusive on this story when and if it breaks—and frankly, when is more likely than if. Agreed?"

Stuart offered tepid words of approval, until he saw Gross's weapon in front of him, at which point his support became more enthusiastic.

"Governor Looney, you will be approached in the very near future about using your position and authority to influence some key legislators on the matter we are discussing. You will agree to do so, but only if you are offered certain remuneration for your efforts."

"In other words," Looney interjected, "I break the law to make law enforcement's case?"

"Yes, Governor. You will be an integral part of our investigation and will be completely exonerated from any alleged criminal activity you are asked to confront so that we can corral those who are actually breaking the law."

"Entrapment," asked the former prosecutor.

"Not from what we have been told by the Justice Department. 'Good government' has its limits. This is an issue that crosses the line."

"I'm good with that, Agent Whitney."

"Thank you, Governor."

"There is one other thing," Whitney added to the conversation with the collective body. "We do have a confidential informant working for us on the inside of this entire operation. In the interest of full disclosure, I have a personal history with one of the subjects of investigation—Jack Adams. Our CI has a history..."

A knock at the door. Agent Gross moved to crack it open. One of his staff members indicated that there was someone there to address the group—someone Agent Whitney had authorized.

As the door flew open, a solitary figure entered the room. Tamara nor Stuart had any idea of who the stranger was.

Rachel spoke to break the awkward silence.

"Governor, Mr. Carroll, may I present to you the CI who will help crush this conspiracy," Rachel was deliberate in her delivery. "Bridget O'Shea."

Chapter 26 — L.A. proved too much...

After Bridget graduated from Berkeley, she moved south to Los Angeles in hopes of succeeding in an acting career. She played the game as best she could by accommodating producers on the casting couch, but no luck. Oh, there was that one-liner she did in a teen slasher film that went straight to DVD.

The waitress was unaware of the dark figure looming in the shadows. As she headed to her car, counting the tips from an evening's work, he sprang from nowhere, grabbed her shoulder and spun her around where she saw the hooded assailant with a hatchet raised above his head.

"Please, don't."

The axe fell and was left in her skull for police as another sign that their elusive prey was still at large.

Certainly not Oscar material. And the ironic fact about it is that had she heeded her own words, "please, don't," she could have avoided a lot of trouble.

The same producer who had her cast as the distressed waitress supplemented his income with pharmaceutical sales — uppers, downers, and everything in between. He was dating Bridget, or at least that's what she told herself. One night at his apartment, their lovemaking was interrupted by lights, sirens, and pounding on the door.

"FBI," said a booming voice on the front stoop.

FBI? Crap. This is serious. Apparently, the pill pushing producer had graduated to the big leagues with the FBI and DEA right outside waiting to take him down as well as anyone else associated with him.

"Here," he pleaded. "Hide this."

He stuffed a small package he pulled from the nightstand into her hands and moved quickly to open the door, knowing full well what awaited him.

At that moment, had she followed her own cinematic line, "please, don't," she might have avoided arrest in the drug bust, avoided the 'deal' offered her to become a confidential informant in exchange for charges against her being dropped, and in the long run, avoided being in Shelbyville to work on bringing down a vote-buying conspiracy that included her friend, Mary Beth.

"Bridget and I go back to Los Angeles when we first started working together," explained Agent Whitney. "As it turns out, we're both home girls—Louisville born and bred. She was important to us in LA by infiltrating the Hollywood drug scene, but more important right now in Kentucky."

"Why's that," Looney wondered aloud.

"One of the other targets of our investigation is a long-time friend of Bridget's," Whitney responded. "In fact, the relationship is so tight, we already have our first win in this battle. Bridget, care to share?"

Bridget had changed clothes after leaving 1 PP. Stylish black T above a black and white hounds tooth skirt, fitted a little too tight for the other ladies in the room, but nicely packaged for the gentlemen, including the asexual Stuart Carroll. She somehow managed to get her hand into a tight, side pocket and retrieved a thumb drive, handing it to Rachel Whitney.

Whitney inserted the drive into a laptop projecting a screen saver on the wall that had been largely ignored.

"Agent Gross, you may want to send out for popcorn and Raisenets. It's show time."

The first file she opened for those gathered in the conference room was audio only. She provided a little play by play...

"Senate President Offutt...

"Speaker Patrick...

"Tony Barrows...

"Two willing hostesses," as she identified Melissa and Melanie.

"Jack Adams," she almost choked on the words.

"And finally, Riley Shaughnessy.

"These are some of the main players. A couple missing in this exchange are Jimmy Flannery, the Governor's Chief of Staff, and Mary Elizabeth Corrigan."

Bridget's eyes welled with tears that she struggled to fight back. She was setting a trap to ensnare a friend she had known for more than two decades. There had to be some way around it, but the answer eluded her. Whitney would be no help. Neither would the reporter or the Lieutenant Governor.

As Whitney prepared to open the second file, which included the Governor at 1 PP, Bridget implored to whatever power on high she could turn to for a solution to help save Mary Beth. She needed a fix. Only one person in all of Kentucky could resolve the situation. She needed Tony on her side — on Mary Beth's side. The job with the law firm was a ruse. She would have time in the days to come to visit with Tony. Looks like another trip to the wine cellar would be in order, away from the prying eyes and ears of Rachel Whitney and her team. First, she had to get through the night with the collective body in the conference room of a roadside motel in Shelbyville.

When Gross insisted on a break to take a smoke, everyone rose to stretch. Bridget asked permission to visit the restroom. It was there that she fidgeted in her skirt for a burner phone Tony had given her along with the thumb drive. She frantically typed a text message to him:

'Must see U ASAP. Tomorrow. UR place. Let me know what time. U, me. No one else.'

Tony was annoyed but intrigued. The text interrupted his movie enjoyment — Yul Brenner and Steve McQueen in the original Magnificent Seven. He broke away long enough to respond:

'MB leaves for work at 8:00. No honeymoon for us! Be here at 10:00. If u r coming from derby city, bring éclairs from Plehn's. I'll have coffee ready.'

That brought back a flood of memories for Bridget. Plehn's was a half-mile from the street where she and Mary Beth grew up. Many a Saturday morning, they would walk to get hot doughnuts washed down with cold milk. As they matured, coffee replaced the milk, but the bakery bonanza remained the same then and now. She looked forward to sharing some of the rich delicacies with Tony.

'Kk' was her only response.

Tony returned to his movie; so did the folks in the Shelbyville conference room.

Chapter 27--Hang 'em High

When Bridget and the others returned to the conference room, things went from bad to worse for Tony, Jack and Mary Beth. But even more detrimental for some of the most powerful men in Frankfort. Audio. Video. A potpourri of incriminating pictures, words and evidence of monetary exchanges.

(As an aside, and purely for information, the most powerful "men" reference is due to the fact that women are grossly underrepresented in the Kentucky legislature. Women comprise only 19 of the 100 House members and 4 of the 38 Senators. None of them are in leadership positions. The highest-ranking woman in state government? Tamara Looney, seated in the room with the FBI going over the who's who of corruption in Frankfort.)

The thumb drive, which had been backed up on four different servers by the Justice Department, was a smoking gun, but only hinted at legislative impropriety. More was needed; something that clearly connected dots to paint a picture of influence peddling. Nothing concrete tied it all together to point to the legislative Hail Mary that Tony was trying to complete for his buddy, and benefactor, Riley Shaughnessy.

Bridget would be helpful in connecting those dots. So, too, would Tamara Looney. Stuart Carroll? He would be along for the ride, he just didn't know where the ride would take him.

Chapter 28 — Plehn and Simple

As promised, Bridget showed up the next morning at 1 PP with éclairs in tow. She let herself in and was greeted by the aroma of rich, dark coffee, which would be a perfect complement to the decadent chocolate pastries.

"Anyone home," she asked, knowing full well that Tony was around.

He lumbered in from the deck and greeted her with a big bear hug.

"Éclairs," he asked with the anticipation of a kid at Christmas.

"One for me, three for you. You're a growing boy."

They sat across from each other at the island and dived into the chocolate delights. Bridget wiped away a little whipped cream from the corner of her mouth and then started a conversation that would change the mood of the morning.

"Tony, you don't know me. I don't know you, but what happened with the whole warrant thing has me spooked. You say it's fishing, but what if it isn't? What if there is something more the police have?"

Big Tony took a bite from his second éclair and mumbled while he chewed, "If they had it, they would have already used it."

Bridget knew better.

"All I ask is that you'll be careful, especially as it concerns Mary Beth. I know you love her; I love her too. If anything does go down, I want to make sure she's protected."

"You're talking about my wife," he chuckled while reaching for his coffee and the third éclair.

'Tony, be serious. This is nothing to laugh about."

"Look, Bridget, You're right. I do love Mary Beth. She is a sweetheart and I wouldn't do anything to put her in jeopardy. But you have to know, I represent a client with a major legislative objective. He has an end game and it's my responsibility to help him win it. Are our tactics ethical? No. Are they legal? Probably not. But I am honor bound to get it done because I gave him my word, and my word is my bond. I intend to keep it that way."

Tony didn't realize it, but he actually had just quoted former U.S. Senator Wendell Ford from a 1986 campaign commercial. It worked for Ford, it will work for Tony.

"Just be careful, Tony. I don't want anything to happen to MB."

"Mary Beth will be okay. I'll make sure of it. Now, I hate to run you off, but Jack and Riley will be here any minute to discuss legislative 'strategy,'" as he used his air quotes.

"Be careful, Tony."

"I will and thanks for the éclairs. Really hit the spot," patting his belly.

A quick peck on his cheek, and Bridget turned to leave. As she opened the door, Shaughnessy and Jack pulled into the driveway together. Bridget waved hello and goodbye while opening her car door.

Oh, to be a fly on the wall, she thought.

Rachel Whitney didn't need a fly on the wall. During the FPD search, officers planted listening devices throughout the house thanks to a court order from a friendly federal judge. Riley, Jack and Tony didn't realize it, but they were about to start connecting dots for Whitney and her team.

Chapter 29 — The countdown is about to begin

The three men greeted each other with handshakes and hugs like long, lost brothers. Ever the host, Tony offered coffee. Riley took him up on it. Jack indicated he may grab a cup, but desperately needed to hit the powder room after the long ride from town. After relieving himself, he renewed his energy with a little coke *sans* bourbon — something he found himself doing more and more to relax amidst the mounting pressures of a legislative strategy clouded by search warrants.

When he rejoined Tony and Riley, he helped himself to a cup of coffee, ambled to the bar, and poured a generous dose of Kahlua.

"A little early, isn't it Jack," voiced a condescending Shaughnessy.

"It's five o'clock somewhere," Tony laughed, although he, too, was becoming more than a little concerned about Jack's consumption of adult beverages, and his increasing reliance on pharmaceuticals — legal and illegal — to help cope with his job. It's one thing to be a political whore; it's another thing entirely to be a drunk, drugged-out political whore.

"Let's get down to business," Tony suggested as he led the way to his home theatre. "It's show time."

Tony started running through an intricate PowerPoint slide show featuring pictures of everyone critical to the end game of repealing right-to-work legislation. Each photo included the subject's name, position in government, specific weaknesses that could be used to Shaughnessy's advantage — like gambling, sexual exploits, substance abuse, or criminal activities up to and including spouse abuse, child abuse, and an uneasy fondness for pornography. To that end, Tony and his extended staff had done a tremendous job researching the individuals who would make or break efforts for a change in labor laws.

Once the list of legislators had been completed, Tony prepared to move on to the executive branch, but Shaughnessy interrupted.

"Where's Peavler," making reference to the Senate Majority Leader. "Without that grandstanding, Bible thumping, TEA drinking, flag waving idiot, we have no shot in the Senate. He'll generate enough bad publicity on this issue to make sure it never sees the light of day in my lifetime."

"Don't worry," Tony started.

"Be happy," Jack piped in. The first words he had spoken since refilling his coffee and Kahlua.

Tony and Riley both shot him death stares.

"As I was saying," Tony continued. "Don't worry. We are still working on Peavler. I know he has a weakness, I just haven't unearthed it yet. When I do, he'll fall in line like a good little soldier. Let's move on to the executive branch."

Jack started to speak but turned his attention to his coffee instead.

The PowerPoint continued in much the same way. Names, research notes, relative position in the RTW debate, etc. It started with the Labor Secretary, Marcia Miller, a retired nurse from a rural hospital organized by the Teamsters. She would be easy. From there, it was up the food chain to COS Jimmy Flannery, an obvious partner in crime, and finally, Damien Lyons himself—the Governor. The elected leader of the Commonwealth of Kentucky. Everyone knew he had opposed right-to-work when it was originally passed. No one knew just how much he opposed it, or more specifically how much money he stood to earn if repeal was successful.

"Very impressive, again," Riley conceded. "But where the hell is Looney. She's worse than Peavler in grabbing headlines. Plus, she's not insane like that little rat bastard."

"We're still working on her," was Tony's only reply.

"You had better get her on board."

"Best case, we will. Worst case, we can neutralize her. I don't know how, yet. We're working on that as well. But we do have a secret weapon."

With that, Tony advanced to the next slide—a dwarf of a man, balding, bearded and bespectacled.

"Who the hell is that," is all Riley could muster.

"Fred Stengel," Tony offered. "Smartest PR man in D.C. with branches in Louisville, Nashville, Montgomery, Atlanta—basically any state where good government can, and often does, succumb to greed and corruption. He could convince legislators to vote against pensions for their own grandmothers. He's that good and he's ours—this time. He did work for the anti-labor guys in passing right-to-work five years ago. Just like his dating preferences, he's a switch hitter on policy issues.

"And that concludes Act One of our play," Tony laughed. "Following intermission, we'll see more specifically what we have on the key players that might convince them to lean our way. And, we'll lay out a timeline of

what needs to happen between now and *sine die*."

The Latin phrase is a reference to adjournment of the legislative session. It is more commonly known in most states as 'let's get the hell out of Dodge.'

The smell of steaks was wafting through the open door to the deck and down into the media center. Marla and her crew were there to clean and, at Tony's instruction, she had fired up the grill for him and his guests. The meal was ready when they made their way to the kitchen. Ribeye's cooked to a medium rare perfection, one of Marla's homemade potato dishes, and grilled asparagus.

"Dig in, boys," Tony suggested. He reached his hand into the fridge and returned with three cold beers. Jack needed no encouragement to take one.

"Here, Riley. Lighten up. It's five o'clock somewhere."

They dived into the steaks like dogs on a meaty bone with the noon news blaring in the background. They spoke very little, with the exception of 'pass the horseradish' and 'can we see what WKYT has on?'

Four Interstate exits up the road, Rachel Whitney and her team had reconvened in the dank hotel conference room. This time, however, they had a receiver and a pair of Bose speakers patched into the audio signals being generated from 1 PP. They had been alerted to the meeting by the FBI crew staked out across the river — the one that discovered Stuart Carroll's attempts at spying on the Barrow's gang.

They had heard the play-by-play that Tony offered in the morning and broke, as Tony and crew had done, for lunch. But theirs was a working lunch — not one to ogle the Bosnian maids who showed up at Tony's in cleaning attire that was a little too short, and a little too tight.

"The targets aren't surprising," Whitney offered. "House and Senate leadership. Members of the Labor and Industry committees. Governor's office. All makes sense.

"What I can't figure out right now is what they have in store for Senator Peavler and Governor Looney. Obviously, Tony has something in mind. We need to find out more — the who, what, when, where…"

She was interrupted, as if on cue, by Bridget O'Shea rejoining the group after her morning jaunt to Frankfort.

"You know we had you under surveillance," SA Gross said sternly.

"I know and that's why I said or did nothing to jeopardize what you all are after," she replied sternly. "I only wanted to let Tony know that I was concerned about Mary Beth and I would tell you the same damned thing right now, next week, next month, or whenever this bullshit goes to trial."

"Both of you calm down," Whitney commanded. "We're a team on this project and we'll play like a team. Nothing rogue. No prima donnas. And no second guessing what we're doing."

Her eyes were fixed on SA Gross at that moment.

"Back to where we were. Bridget, we can give you all of the information we have so you're not left in the dark on anything. But we need your help on two critical matters — what Barrows has planned for Senate Peavler and Governor Looney. Peavler, we could give a shit about. If he goes down, it's probably a blessing for everyone in the state. Looney, on the other hand, is one of the white hats and we need to protect her as much as possible because of her willingness to help with the investigation.

"We need you to get information from Tony or, our friend, Jack Adams. Can you do that?"

"You want me to prostitute myself for your investigation," Bridget was incensed.

"On the contrary, Bridget," was Whitney's response. "I would much prefer you get the information standing on your feet rather than lying on your back. Less likely to be challenged as coercion or entrapment."

Bridget huffed, but offered no additional response.

"You said yourself that you wanted to protect Mary Beth. If they plan to use her in some capacity to win over Looney and Peavler, she could get hurt. You can stop that. All that's needed is to win Tony's confidence or, unfortunately for him, get Jack just high enough to spill his guts, and we'll have everything we need."

The exchange between Bridget and Rachel had devolved into cold silence, which was interrupted by the clanking of dishes coming over the speakers.

"To the Bat Cave," Tony ordered.

The three men made their way back to the home theatre for Act Two of Tony's show and tell. Jack made a second stop in the powder room along the way where he did a second line of coke to get him through the boredom that faced him.

All ears in Shelbyville turned to the speakers.

"Tony, before we get started, I want your assurance that Peavler and Looney will play ball," Shaughnessy insisted. "The last thing we need is a couple of media hounds screaming for headlines about corruption in state government."

"It's under control, or it will be before we kick off this campaign publicly. You have my word."

The afternoon was most entertaining for a voyeur like Riley Shaughnessy. Tony's presentation not only included a description of what they had on each of the major players, but also audio and video of them in compromising positions that would certainly encourage their support for the RTW repeal initiative.

From the putting green shenanigans to the tryst in the trees to the Vargas girl presentations, the evidence was compelling and overwhelming. There was also a video recording of Governor

Lyons with both his press secretary and his Secretary of Economic Development during a European recruiting mission three-way. And it's safe to say that the mission position is not what they were demonstrating. Thank you to Evelyn Ward for including a camera with your press credentials on the trip.

"Digital recordings are such a wonder," a thought Tony blurted aloud.

"Yes, they are," Rachel Whitney responded from 30 miles away.

The afternoon droned on. Once you've seen one middle-aged white guy with a rainbow of sweet, young things, you've see them all. Tony thought it important, though, that Jack and Riley knew how much work had gone into this fact finding and what the Achilles Heel was for each of the major players in this game of thorny issues.

As the last slide faded to black, Tony announced that it actually *was* five o'clock! The three climbed the stairs to a first floor that was immaculately cleaned by Marla and crew. A tray of cheeses, fruits and crackers was left on the island.

"Riley, my man, one more thought before Happy Hour. We'll discuss it in more detail tomorrow," he teased as he reached a spreader for the brie with one paw while a slice of apple occupied his other. "Fred thinks we ought to announce this all on Labor Day—the whole kit and caboodle. We have our sponsor identified. We take advantage of a slow news weekend. We announce our efforts in a series of press conferences and define what the repeal looks like. We strike while the other side is sleeping over the holiday weekend. We take it to the masses starting then and keep the drumbeat up until the session starts in January."

"Tony, Labor Day is only three weeks away."

"And that gives us three weeks to turn Peavler and Looney, get the rest of the players in line with us, lay out the game plan for Lyons, and get the money from your guys to assure that we have the resources in place to make this all happen."

Jack had already occupied himself at the bar, but still managed to listen a bit through his haze.

"Tony, I have an idea about Peavler," he muttered.

Shaughnessy and Barrows turned to Jack. Is the wayward quarterback about ready to call an audible?

"Before I got into this shit storm, I was engaged to a beautiful young lady named Rachel Whitney. I loved her. She loved me. We were going to be a great couple until her father and my grandfather sent the whole thing spiraling out of control."

Neither Riley nor Tony had ever heard Jack talk about his past with such candor. It was usually confined to 'guess who has a mole on her twat" or something equally as crude.

"She was black, which didn't set well with my grandfather. Obviously, her dad was black, too. He started shaking the branches of our family tree and soon discovered that granddad's ancestors were big into the KKK in Kentucky. And old Clement himself was a major funder of the Klan today."

"All, nice, Jack, but what the hell does it mean for us," Shaughnessy was growing more impatient with Jack's whatever-induced ramblings.

"Darren Peavler is on the board of my grandfather's energy company," which got the Tony's attention. "He represents Knott County Kentucky Kiln Company, a group that produces fire bricks and other clay-based materials."

"Jack, you're starting to bore me," Riley said exuding an increasing level of impatience.

"Don't you get it," Jack asked Riley, who apparently was not adept at problem solving. "Knott County Kentucky Kiln Company. KCKKC. Knock out the C-C for Clement Combs, who has majority stock in the outfit, and what's left? KKK."

"Peavler is in the Klan," Tony was dumbfounded. "You know that for a fact?"

"I can give you the name of the dry cleaner who does his sheets," Jack said sarcastically.

"Then we don't need to sic Mary Beth on him?"

"Heavens, no," Jack slurred.

"Save her for a rainy day, and pray that it doesn't rain," he offered as an afterthought.

A long pause followed at 1 PP and at the hotel in Shelbyville.

"So, what about Looney?" Riley remained impatient on the status of the Lieutenant Governor. "How do we get her on board."

Tony was riding a bit of a high now that Jack had opened the door to winning over Peavler.

"Well, it's one down and one to go. Contrary to the old saying, 'the way to a man's heart is *not* through his stomach,' it's really through his pecker. Looney doesn't have a pecker, but her husband does. A friend of ours has indicated that she will do anything to protect a member of our family. This could be right up her alley."

All ears in Frankfort waited for Tony to break the suspense. All eyes in Shelbyville turned to Bridget.

At that point, Rachel was dialing the phone. It was Tamara Looney's private number.

"This is Rachel Whitney. I need to speak with Governor Looney right now. She'll know what it's about. Please put me through."

Once she accepted the call, Looney inquired as to what was happening.

"Governor," only two questions. "Can your husband be trusted? And would he like to have a sexual encounter with an attractive brunette?"

Looney was stunned.

The collective body in Shelbyville was smiling, except for Bridget.

"Standing on my feet rather than lying on my back? What is this bitch up to?"

Labor Day is only three weeks away.

Chapter 29—It was a dark and stormy night

"May I put you on speaker," Rachel asked the Lieutenant Governor.

"Of course."

"Governor, with me is Special Agent Walker Gross, who you met last night. Also here is Tom Mayfield from our technical unit. He has been responsible for electronic surveillance of Barrows, Adams, and company, including Riley Shaughnessy. Special Agents Jason Todd and Jeremy Staton are here as well. They have been eyes and ears on the ground since this investigation started. And finally, Bridget O'Shea, who you met last night."

"What, if anything, is new?"

"A lot, ma'am."

Rachel went on to recap the day of eavesdropping, including the Reader's Digest version of the players, the timeline being proposed, and the concerns Shaughnessy had about Looney's willingness to get on board.

"And what does all of this have to do with my husband and an encounter with some bimbo?"

Bridget bristled a bit. She knew she was the bimbo that Looney was referring to even though Agent Whitney had not yet laid out the plan.

"Governor, with apologies in advance for the crude language, Barrows indicated to the labor leader that the way to a man's heart if through his pecker. We have someone we can put on the case, but ma'am, know in advance, it will be a ploy. Nothing will happen. We can only do it if your husband is willing and if he can be trusted."

Silence.

"Governor, are you there?"

More silence, until finally…

"More details, Agent Whitney."

Rachel explained what she had cooked up on the spot. Bridget would seduce Dr. Tunie under the guise of working on Tony's behalf. The whole thing would be captured on video from the time they first meet until they disappear in a Frankfort hotel room.

Bridget hung on Whitney's every word just as Looney was.

"Ms. O'Shea will be our bait."

A description that pissed off Bridget, but her concern for Mary Beth restrained her from walking away.

"She will approach your husband in a predetermined place and gradually seduce him to the point where he will agree to ask her to a room. Once there, our surveillance will continue in case Ms. O'Shea has a change in heart."

Bridget huffed again.

"But Barrows' listening opportunity will be lost because of a 'technical malfunction.' He will have nothing but photos and audio from the bar. We are the only ones who will have eyes and ears on the room. All your husband has to do is escort Ms. O'Shea to the room and then wait until morning. We will make sure he's comfortable. Ms. O'Shea will excuse herself to an adjoining room.

"In the morning, your husband will order room service for two. We have a suspicion that Barrows has contacts in the hotel, so it's likely that the room service attendant will be equipped with a camera to record the 'love birds' in the room. Ms. O'Shea will join your husband before the food is delivered wearing a strapless bikini so that as much skin as possible will be exposed to the delivery guy as she draws the matelassé coverlet and sheet up to her chest. We suspect he will be snapping pictures on some hidden device. We want them to be as provocative as possible to satisfy Barrows' intent that something sinister has happened without compromising your husband's integrity."

Looney listened on, as did Bridget since this was her role.

"Once room, service has been delivered, we wait for an acceptable amount of time to pass before your husband and Ms. O'Shea leave the room—separately. Barrows will pick up his surveillance then."

"Can he be trusted?"

"No question. I'll explain as much as I can without putting the investigation in jeopardy. But why would someone as beautiful as Ms. O'Shea give a second thought to Dave? I love him, but we click at a soulful level as much as a physical level. Won't Barrows be curious as to why he would pick up a strange woman and escort her to a hotel room?"

"He's not picking her up; she's picking him up. And Governor, please know it will all be an act, but he needs to be vulnerable — like talking about how frigid his wife is and how the thrill of their—your—relationship had disintegrated. Can he do that?"

"He can and he will. Once he knows the magnitude of this investigation, he will be an award-winning thespian. I'm sure of that."

Two days later, the plan was put in place. Looney had briefed her husband on what he could expect while visiting the bar at the Capital Plaza during some continuing education conference. But there was a complicating factor—unexpected by everyone involved in the investigation.

As he sat in the hotel bar waiting for Bridget, Jimmy Flannery, the Governor's chief of staff, spotted him across the room and made his way over.

"Dave, honey, imagine you here, now. Why, I haven't seen you since that glorious night at the Omni during the Southern Legislative Conference in Atlanta."

"Oh, Jimmy. Good to see you. It *has* been a while."

Shakiness had taken over his vocal cords as he tried to make idle conversation with Flannery. The situation was now incredibly uneasy for Tony, who was listening in at 1 PP and for Rachel who was listening in at the Shelbyville hotel. Dave had no idea that Flannery would be in the picture, nor did Whitney. Nor did anyone else for that matter, including Tamara Looney.

Get Bridget in there now!

It wasn't spoken, but the sentiment was shared by the FBI, the Lieutenant Governor, and, by an odd turn of events, Tony and company. The last thing anyone needed was Flannery trying to score with the Lieutenant Governor's husband. He needed to go away. Bridget needed to step in. Before Jimmy was able to dig deeper into Dr. Tunie's intentions, Bridget appeared from nowhere and cozied up to Dave. He took his cue and cozied up to her.

"Jimmy, let me get back to you tomorrow," he whispered. "I'm sure this distraction could last for a little while."

Tunie offered a wink of confidence; Flannery rolled his eyes, and walked away.

Bridget climbed onto Dave's lap. They could hear an approaching storm—lightening, thunder, and torrential rain.

"Care to join me upstairs to ride out the weather," Dave asked just loud enough for all around to hear. He had determined that enough time had passed, and enough bourbon had been consumed, that the conversation needed to adjourn to a more private setting.

"Let's go, sugar," was Bridget's matching-volume response.

Governor Looney would have to deal with why her husband had been approached by Jimmy Flannery. Flannery would have to deal with why his advances to a normally receptive Dave Tunie had been rebuffed. Tunie would have to deal with how he will explain the Flannery conversation to his wife. Bridget would have to deal with how she could and would express her love for Mary Beth.

Labor Day is less than three weeks away.

Chapter 30 — Technology is great — when it works

"Dammit," Tony screamed from his vantage point at 1 PP listening to the wire on Bridget that went suddenly silent when she and Dave Tunie entered his room. "What the fuck is going on here?"

His question was posed to no one, and everyone — especially Arty West, the computer geek who kept 1 PP wired. West scrambled on his laptop trying to determine what had happened and why the bug went dead.

"If we don't have sound or pictures, all we have is Bridget's word and that's shit."

Tony was screaming at anyone within earshot. This was a pivotal moment in the labor campaign — something that could take out Tamara Looney. But all they had now was scratchy audio from the bar and a few pictures Bridget managed to take with her phone.

"Is he in a fucking bunker? What the hell is going on."

After finally resigning himself to the fact that nothing more would be seen or heard that night, Tony made a call to his source in the hotel to make sure any and all room service orders to Dr. Tunie's suite would be captured on video or in photos.

That was his first call.

The second went to Jack Adams.

"Jack, I'm trying to get everything in place for the big party. You said you could prove that Peavler is a Klan member. Then do it! I need hard, fast documentation, and I need it as soon as you can get it to me. Labor Day is creeping up on us."

The third call went to Mary Beth.

"Hi, honey. I'm home."

They both laughed at his Ozzie and Harriet moment.

"Mary Beth, we have Peavler — or at least that's what Jack says. We have Looney, or we will after Bridget finishes her assignment tonight. We have leadership in the House and Senate. We have the Governor and his staff. We have everything we need. So why am I calling you?"

MB was wondering the same thing.

"Our PR guy wants to launch this attack on Labor Day weekend. It's a time for politicians to take center stage, not a time for political whores like yours truly to be anywhere in sight. The long and short of it is do you want to go to Florida with me?"

Mary Beth was stunned. Yes, they were married in the legal sense of things, but Tony had never come on to her since that initial encounter in the Annex cafeteria so many years ago.

"Tony, I love you like a brother," she finally got a few words out. "But I don't know…"

"Shit, MB. I'm not trying to get in your pants. I need to get the hell out of Frankfort for a while and thought you might want to come along to enjoy the sea breeze with me. Hell, bring Bridget if you want. I know you all have a lot in common. I just wanted some company because I need to get out of here and wanted a friendly face to be with me."

Mary Beth broke her silence with a simple, "OK."

"Great. I'll get travel details worked out. You think Bridget can break away from her law firm for a week? I need to know to book air fare. Or hell, we can drive down. Pensacola isn't that far away. We can stay near Flora Bama. Right on the Gulf. Maybe wander over to Gulf Shores for a day to visit a friend of mine."

Gulf Shores? Bridget? Those two nouns hadn't been together for MB in years. The memories flooded her senses—all of them from the smell of the ocean salt and sound of waves crashing on the beach to the taste of Bridget's lips, and the touch of her silky skin.

"Earth to Mary Beth. Come in Mary Beth."

Tony's taunt jarred her back to the here and now.

"Marvelous idea, Mr. Barrows. Let's get away as soon as we can."

"Very good, Mrs. Barrows. You check with your companion to see if she's available."

"Oh, I'm sure she can work it out," MB said with a hopeful smile. This is a reunion she would be looking forward to.

In the Capital Plaza Hotel, Bridget was alone in her room. Next door was Dr. Tunie, no doubt trying to figure out how the Flannery conversation could be explained to his wife. A personal burner phone rang. It was a phone that the FBI didn't know about; Tony didn't know about; her law firm didn't know about; only Mary Beth.

They were both pretty confident that the feds had not tapped the phone, but they were also quite sure they had wired the room. Bridget spoke in hushed tones as she answered with a weak, "hello."

"Want to return to the scene of the crime," MB offered in a code that only Bridget would understand. "The big guy and I are leaving for a week. Care to join us—I hope!"

"Anything for you and your hubby," Bridget responded with a hint of trepidation. "Count me in."

She wanted more information, but this was not the time to ask for it. MB wanted more information, but Tony was on to the next shiny object vying for his attention—the hotel security camera that his guy had hacked. He was playing and rewinding the brief encounter between Dave Tunie and Jimmy Flannery.

He thought to himself that Bridget would be the first trap set to bring Governor Looney on board. But Looney's own husband and the Governor's chief of staff offered a totally new perspective on things. That could also work to his benefit and the benefit of his client, Riley Shaughnessy.

"This is good," he told himself as he sipped on Blanton's neat.

"This is shit," Agent Whitney screamed from her Shelbyville hotel conference center. "As soon as they check out tomorrow, I want Tunie here with his wife. This crap ends now before it compromises everything else we're doing."

Nightfall brought with it a full moon peering down on the many players involved in this escapade. Audio tracks were rolling; video was being shot; code was being spoken. And far off in Pikeville, Clement Combs sat quietly in an overstuffed club chair pondering the world through a prism of bourbon. He and the many companies he owned were staunch supporters of right to work. Jack had confided to him, during an Oxy experience, that his client would be going for repeal.

Old Clement sensed something would be happening soon — probably around Labor Day. That's what he would do if he were in charge. He needed more information. It couldn't come from Jack — too obvious. It couldn't come from Tony because of some bad blood between the two after Jack was made a named partner, wiping out any chance of him joining Yellow Creek Energy. Clement didn't know where to turn, so he thought he would reach out to his long-time friend who had been true over the years — FBI Special Agent Jason Todd.

The "negress," Whitney, controlled investigations about federal offenses. Agent Todd thought, as did Clement, that the feds were overreaching the government's authority. He reported back to Clement what had transpired so far in the FBI probe, including the increasingly fragile antics of his grandson, Jack Adams. This would be a long night, one of many to come.

Chapter 31 — Proud to be a Coal Miner's Son

Otis Todd was a coal miner. He started working in deep mines when he was 15 and lied about his age so he could help support his family — mother, disabled father, and three siblings. By the time he turned 24, he knew as much about underground mining as anyone twice his age. This gift didn't escape the watchful eyes of Clement Combs, who brought the young man from Owsley County to Pike County to be a foreman for one of Yellow Creek Energy's deep mines.

Todd eventually married and had three children — two girls and a boy, Jason, so named because of his father's fascination with Greek and Roman mythology. Even though he had dropped out of school in the sixth grade, Otis was an avid reader who wore out nearly every book in the county library. He loved biographies of famous people, tolerated the occasional bit of fiction, and devoured anything he could find on ancient mythology.

Jason led the Argonauts; his Jason would be a leader, too. Clement Combs agreed and took the Todd family under his wings.

As deep mining gave way to cheaper surface mining, Clement followed suit and named Otis as his superintendent of all the new strip mining operations he opened in Floyd, Pike and Martin counties. Clement and Yellow Creek became more successful, so, too, did Otis and his family — until tragedy struck.

Otis was visiting a Martin County mine near Inez when his pickup was pummeled by a truck laden with coal. Afterward, Clement became even more involved with the Todd family, which included paying Otis's widow a monthly "pension" to help her make ends meet. He fed and clothed the children throughout their school careers. And because he took a special liking to young Jason, he made sure that he didn't want for anything.

Centre College undergrad — Clement paid for it.

University of Kentucky Law School — Clement paid for it.

The old man even pulled a few political strings to get Jason accepted into the FBI academy, where he excelled. After a few years of chasing bad guys in Wisconsin, where he never got accustomed to the accent, he returned to the white-collar crime unit in Kentucky. He rekindled his relationship with Clement, who had all but given up on Jack as his successor. Jason was the heir apparent and he knew it. That's why he would do anything within reason to help Clement.

He considered periodic updates about the ongoing investigation into government corruption within reason — especially since it included Jack.

Chapter 32—(Fill in the Blank) Comes in Threes

The expression is as old as time. Good things come in threes. Bad luck comes in threes. Misfortune comes in threes. Death comes in threes.

Sometimes, though, it's a combination.

First, Agent Todd awoke on the morning following the Dave Tunie-Bridget O'Shea debacle at the Capital Plaza to find that his mentor, Clement, had made a significant deposit into a bank account that only he and Mr. Combs knew about.

Second, Tony called about travel plans for himself, Mary Beth, and Bridget. Flight out of Lexington to Atlanta and on to Mobile. Rental car to Orange Beach. Six nights in a luxury condo overlooking the Gulf. He couldn't wait to leave the oppressive heat and humidity in Kentucky for a nice sea breeze on the Gulf.

Finally, the cage match with Tamara Looney, Dave Tunie, and Rachel Whitney. You might not have heard of Michael Buffer. He's the guy who coined—and later trademarked the phrase, 'Let's get ready to rumble.' He may have never visited Shelbyville, Kentucky, but his signature statement could not have been more appropriate.

After an ever-so-brief exchange of pleasantries, the bedlam erupted much as it had with the O'Shea's and Corrigan's in Alabama.

"What in the hell was that?"

"Are you internationally trying to blow this investigation."

"I never had any idea you would…"

"I'm sorry. I didn't mean to…"

"This could get you in hot water with more than your wife."

"I'm sorry."

"WAIT."

The last word slightly below a scream on a decibel scale came from Tamara Looney.

"Agent Whitney, did you get what you needed from my husband?"

"Yes, Governor, we did."

"Dr. Tunie," this was going to be bad news. "Did anything happen during this undercover investigation Agent Whitney or I should be aware of?"

"Tamara, please!"

"Did anything happen during this assignment that we should be concerned about in terms of compromising this investigation?"

"Tamara, honey, let's talk. But not here."

"Dr. Tunie, do not call me Tamara and do not call me honey. For you, now and forever more, I will be Governor Looney. And we have nothing to talk about other than terms of the divorce."

With that, the good doctor burst into tears and lowered his face into two waiting hands.

"Dr. Tunie, you will leave for Florida by the end of the day to attend to ailing parents. That's your story and you're going to stick by it, or I'll expose you and your boyfriend as far and wide as I can reach. And you know that the media hounds love me."

More tears. More sniffling. More sobbing. Rachel Whitney was speechless at what she was witnessing. Yes, she had a monumental split with Jack Adams. But this was the Lt. Governor dressing down her prominent physician husband while she was making every attempt possible to maintain the integrity of the investigation. Once a prosecutor, always a prosecutor.

"When this inquiry is over, you can return to Louisville if you want, but you will always be looking over your shoulder to see if I'm coming after you. So that may not be advisable. If I were you, I'd go back to reestablish a practice in Atlanta, or stay in Vero Beach to be close to your folks. Your days as the fair-haired boy at U of L are over.

"Agent Whitney, is there somewhere you and I can retreat to while we leave Dr. Tunie to mourn his personal and professional losses?"

"Upstairs. My suite. We're safe there. Already swept for bugs."

"Then, my dear Rachel, let's away to continue our planning," her demeanor was calmer and more condescending. She used a final closing statement, just as she would have during trial. "Dr. Tunie, remember the personal bourbon trail I made for you? Remember how you enjoyed the sweet taste of the whiskey against the salt of my skin? Remember how we made love that night? Well think of that every time Jimmy Flannery has his cock up your ass! Goodbye, Dr. Tunie. If you're not out of our house by the time I get home this afternoon, I'll call the police. Safe travels, asshole."

And like that, it was over. Tunie continued to weep. Whitney and Looney took the elevator to the third floor and the suite with a small table in the living area. Once settled into their chairs with a fresh cup of coffee for each from the hotel Keurig, Whitney spoke first.

"Governor Looney, I am so sorry that this investigation drove a wedge between you and your husband. Is there anything I can do, that the FBI can do to patch things up?"

"Rachel, darling, don't fret. I long suspected something was different with Dave, but never had any evidence. Last night just offered up the ammunition I needed. It's not the FBI's fault, and certainly not yours. Let it go and let's concentrate on what's important—bringing down this snake pit of corruption."

Whitney nodded, and the two women carried on their discussion.

Downstairs, Dave Tunie composed himself enough to walk out of the hotel and into a state police SUV used by the Lt. Governor's detail. Home for a quick shower; pack the essentials; and then off to Florida to be with his parents at the Kentucky Club in Vero. Not what he had imagined at this stage in his career. But meeting Jimmy Flannery the night before in the hotel bar was not in the game plan either.

As the trooper drove silently toward the Lt. Governor's house on Brownsboro Road in Louisville, Tunie punched in a number on his cell phone.

"Jimmy, she knows."

"Calm down, Dave. She knows what?"

"She knows about you and me. She knows what sort of relationship we have. She blames me for compromising the inves..."

He caught himself and stopped short.

"Compromising what?"

Silence.

"Compromising what, Dave?"

Recovering rather quickly lest he face the wrath of the FBI and his soon-to-be estranged wife, "Compromising the investment of time and energy we have made to get her elected to higher office."

"Get over yourself. I'm sorry, my friend, but Tamara Looney will never hold another elected office in this state. She has pissed off too many of the wrong people for that to happen."

Tunie sat in silence, broken only by his weak, "I have to go."

The Brownsboro Road house was unassuming from the outside. A late 50's ranch on a two-acre lot. Inside, though, was a page out of *Southern Living* with all of the accoutrements and trappings of the one percent.

Dave made his way through the antique-lined entryway and living area to the kitchen — his kitchen. Although a skilled physician by trade, he was equally adept in cooking masterpieces of his own design. His motto was 'like speed limit signs, recipes are a suggestion.'

He sat on one of the barstools at the island and looked into 'his' kitchen. Nothing, absolutely nothing was second rate. He did wonder, however, why he and his wife spent as much as they had on their first house to buy Thermador equipment that didn't function well in a working kitchen. Great form; lousy function.

As he pondered the appliances' shortcomings, he removed a knife from its block. The Henckels' eight-inch blade was honed to perfection, cold and hard to his touch. He retired to the pool deck out back, knife in hand. As he took a seat on one of the chaise lounges, he looked skyward; asked for forgiveness; and plunged the knife into his abdomen in a Kentucky version of hari-kari.

No note. None would be needed for the grieving widow, who became more of a media darling than she was previously. The questions persisted, but her tried and true response was that her husband had been battling depression for a long time and it seemed to get worse rather than better despite treatment.

She was despondent.

Jimmy Flannery was devastated.

Chapter 33 — Let the Games Begin

Dave Tunie's death was the lead story in every daily newspaper and for the talking-head TV anchors throughout the state, as well as surrounding markets in Cincinnati, Evansville, Nashville, Huntington, and Knoxville. The coverage quoted Tamara Looney, chapter and verse, about her husband succumbing to the demons of depression. The timing of his death was a godsend for the media because it came during the political purgatory between the annual Fancy Farm picnic where campaigns come to live or die, and Labor Day, which had historically been a Democratic touchstone.

Fred Stengel wanted to make sure this Labor Day celebration resurrected the glory days of unions at the expense of right-to-work advocates. The media played right along because taking up the baton in support of repealing RTW was the grieving widow, Tamara Looney. She "pulled herself together" well enough to do a fly-around in the state on Labor Day weekend voicing her position on why the legislature should repeal or amend right-to-work legislation. Her script came right off the pages of the Stengel strategy manual. Her impassioned plea came because of a commitment she made to her late husband, who had grown up in family where the patriarch was an avowed Teamster and, later, UAW member.

Of course, the real reason behind her public posturing was a late-night visit from Jimmy Flannery and Damien Lyons at her capitol office. They outlined the overarching game plan, impressed upon her the value of her support, and then played a video file that recounted her husband's dalliance at the Capital Plaza. She feigned shock and surprise. Little did the Governor and his COS know that she had helped set the wheels in motion to compromise her husband — her late husband.

As the video did an abrupt transition to black, the Governor asked, "Tamara, do we have your support?"

"And what if I say 'no?'"

Flannery jumped in, "Then, Governor Looney, I'm afraid copies of this video will find their way into every media outlet in the state, as well as many at the national level, including conservative bloggers who would like nothing more than to eat you for lunch."

"Extortion, in other words?"

"Your definition, not ours," Lyons offered. "Look at it this way. If you do what we're asking, you will become even more of a rock star with the media than you are now. I can run for the Senate next year to replace that old fart, McDougal, and when I leave, you become Governor. With the stance you have taken — or will take — on right to work, you'll be a shoo-in to win the seat outright during the next election and the sky is the limit for you afterwards."

"I shouldn't," Tamara said, followed by a long pause. "But I will — on one condition."

"Governor, you're in no position to make this conditional…"

"Shut up. Jimmy." Lyons turned a stern eye on his chief of staff and then back to his Lt. Governor. "Tell me, Tamara. What is your condition?"

"I want Tony Barrows to go down."

The Governor and his COS looked at each other, back at Tamara Looney, and back at each other before either could muster the words to speak.

"Why? Why Tony?" That was all Lyons could say.

"I can't prove it, but I know he's bad," Tamara said without any reservation. "I suspect he set my husband up with that hooker in the bar…"

Jimmy Flannery retreated a bit from his prior bravado.

"I know he has been working on this issue for Riley Shaughnessy. And I know he has no moral compass to guide him. He's everything bad that we need to eliminate in Frankfort. That is my condition. He goes down."

Without hesitation, Lyons nodded an emphatic yes. Flannery was less emphatic, but offered his endorsement. Tony was completely unaware of the conversation. He was off in Florida with Mary Beth and Bridget. His only notice came in a cryptic text from Flannery.

LG is on board. Coming soon to a TV near you.

That's all he needed. He had assurance that the sole remaining obstacle to his plan was now on his side. The countdown to the start of the legislative session was about to begin. The House was his; the Senate would not be as easy, but would be winnable; the grieving widow in the Lt. Governor's office would give the issue standing with the public; the Governor was already warming up his writing hand to sign the bill. Nothing stood in his way.

After he read Jimmy's text, he called out to Mary Beth and Bridget, who were doing a little skinny dipping in the pool, "Ladies, we have something to celebrate. Come join me on the balcony."

They took turns drying each other by the pool, threw on swim covers, and rode the elevator up to Tony's condo. He was already on the lanai with drink in hand; they scurried to join their host.

"To us!" Tony was his boisterous self.

"What are we celebrating," MB asked.

"Ladies, mark this day on your calendar for all time. This is the night that we start on a road that will lead to us to victory for our client, but more importantly, put us on the map for any issue that comes down the pike in the future. We didn't win the Powerball, but this is the next best thing!"

Tony didn't have ears on the conversation between Lyons and Looney, which would have dramatically tempered his celebration. Nor did he have a bug planted on Jack, who at that very moment, was washing down a fist full of pain meds with a shot of Knob Creek. As a result, he didn't know that Jack's companion was an old friend from Pike County who turned informant when the FBI and DEA busted her beau for trafficking. And he didn't have a wire on Bridget or Mary Beth — where could he hide one while they were swimming nude?

But Bridget had a bug in the suite.

Agent Todd had one on the Pike County informant who was making every effort to keep Jack from overdosing.

Tamara Looney had one concealed in a brooch her grandmother had given her.

And Rachel Whitney had a ringside seat in the Shelbyville conference room to hear all of the conversations. She took a sip of bitter coffee and chased it with the sweet chocolate of an éclair from Plehn's that one of her agents had brought her that morning. The pastry brought a smile to her lips; the patsies made the smile much broader.

Chapter 34 — September; the Clock Starts

Tamara Looney became even more of a media darling than she was before, just as Damien Lyons had predicted. Her Labor Day Weekend fly-around started in Louisville at Bowman Field aboard a Piper Matrix — large enough to accommodate her, her press assistant, reporters from the Lexington and Louisville newspapers, and Riley Shaughnessy — his union contacts would be responsible for turning out crowds.

From Louisville to Ashland, Hazard, Somerset, Lexington, Bowling Green, Owensboro, Paducah, and finally Hopkinsville — because of its proximity to Fort Campbell, which gave her an opportunity to "commend the brave men and women stationed here who are honor bound to preserve our freedom." That comment played well locally, but also received attention in Nashville — the closest metro market.

Her ascent to the Governor's Mansion was becoming a reality as fast as the military jets that screamed overhead at the conclusion of her remarks.

As the plane made its final approach to Louisville, Looney pulled Shaughnessy close to her. She whispered loud enough for him to hear above the hum of the engine and squawking of the radio but subdued enough that other passengers made no notice.

"We're done now, Riley. I don't ever want to see you again. You disgust me. I set this charade in motion like a good little trooper in support of her Governor, but I'm finished. The rest is up to you and your band of hoodlums, like Tony Barrows. Don't call me. Don't write me. Anything I do from here on out will be at my discretion. Understand?"

Shaughnessy nodded with a stunned look on his face. He understood completely. The rest was up to him—and Tony.

The media coverage was everything and more the cast of characters could have hoped for. Tamara Looney, the grieving widow, put personal sadness aside to rally Kentucky's working men and women to exert pressure on the legislature to repeal or amend right-to-work legislation. As was the case with Dave Tunie's death, she was front page news and the lead TV story in every Kentucky market as well as those in neighboring states. She even got a mention in *USA Today*, as Tony found out when he picked up a copy at the Pensacola airport. He was on his way home with Bridget and Mary Beth in tow. Two weeks in the land of sun and sand had energized him for the fight to come.

He made mental notes on his game plan constantly. Revisions here. New approaches there. Safeguards that needed to be put in place. Contingencies for anything that might deviate from the master plan. His mind worked non-stop on the trip home—confident that all would be okay as a result of the statewide initiative Looney had launched; wary that something unforeseen could bring the entire effort crashing down around him.

But Tony was a fixer and this issue had been adequately fixed. Or so he thought. The bug that Bridget had placed in the condo was now residing in Tony's watch—a lookalike Rolex Bridget had switched when Tony went out for a final morning jog before returning to Kentucky. The only time he removed that Rolex was when he ran, when he showered, and when he swam. Those were all solitary activities, so Rachel Whitney didn't risk missing out on much.

The flight home was uneventful—as all flights should be. When he and the girls deplaned in Lexington, it was a different story. Waiting for them at the luggage carousel was Stuart Carroll.

Stuart was incensed that he was not included on the Lt. Governor's fly-around. He knew as much as she did about the FBI probe, and yet he was shut out. Confronting Tony about the master plan would be his way of evening the score with Tony, but also with Agent Whitney. He could visualize the headline as he saw Tony, Mary Beth and Bridget descend on the escalator.

Frankfort lobbyist tied to federal probe.

That headline would have to wait.

As he made eye contact with Tony, a team of TSA agents surrounded Stuart and whisked him away. Tony laughed at the idea that his namby nemesis had been detained by authorities. He grabbed his suitcase, as did Mary Beth and Bridget. They were out the door and on their way to Tony's car as Stuart loudly protested on his route to a holding cell on the airport's second floor.

Tony and his companions sped off in his Jag.

Stuart continued his vocal protests about freedom of the press, first amendment rights, unlawful detainment, and other constitutional violations when Rachel Whitney and Tamara Looney entered the room.

Whitney's eyes were laser focused on Stuart as he rose to his feet to continue his protest. If looks could kill, he would have died on the spot. Tamara Looney again came to his rescue with a directive she had used previously, only this time, more emphatic.

"Stuart, sit down and shut the fuck up."

Tamara and Rachel tried as best they could to assure Stuart that he would have an exclusive on this story as they had promised. But if he pulled another stunt like the one just played out, all deals were off. He would be denied any access to important information, and his story would be a rewrite of something the *Herald* or *Courier* would break. He would be rewarded for his patience, but his patience needed to be unwavering.

He agreed to be a good boy — reluctantly, but he did agree.

His reward was not long in coming. At 1:00 in the morning, he got an anonymous phone call from someone who sounded suspiciously like Rachel Whitney.

"Call the Pikeville Medical Center. Ask about Jack Adams' condition. Ask if the tox screen showed whether the pills were Oxy or Xanax. Run with the story — including all of the background you can find on his family."

"But wait," Stuart was stumbling to find the right questions to ask. "Why am I interested in Jack Adams? Why is this important to anyone? Why should I..."

He never finished his sentence. The female voice on the phone interjected and simply said, "Trust me."

With that, she hung up. As he sat bewildered by what had just transpired, his groggy thoughts were interrupted with a ping on his phone that an email had just arrived. Sender unknown. Subject line—Jack Adams. Attachments included pictures from the ER showing Jack being bagged for oxygen, a dossier on Clement Combs, correspondence from Sen. Peavler to Clement about Klan activities, and a copy of the statement Jack's companion had given to Pikeville police about their afterhours activities.

The single sentence in the body of the email was all Stuart needed to dive into the investigation of Jack and his brush with death by overdose.

This is a preview of things to come – if you're patient.

Chapter 35 – October

By the time October rolls around, two certainties usually reverberate throughout the Commonwealth: 1) football fans put the current season behind them and look forward to a new start next year, and 2) basketball fans start counting down the days to the tipoff of another run at a national championship.

This year was different. The football team was off to a 6-0 start for the first time since Bear Bryant was the coach in the 1950s. The basketball team would hope to be a .500 squad after NCAA sanctions wiped out the newest crop of one-and-dones, leaving only three scholarship players and a bunch of walk-ons.

The world was off its axis.

Frankfort was not to be spared.

Even though the candidate filing deadline was months away, Damien Lyons announced that he would take on Micha McDougal for the U.S. Senate seat. The early decision afforded Lyons an opportunity to raise significant amounts of cash for his exploratory committee – all of which would be needed he if he had any shot at upending the four-term Senator. While Lyons set out in pursuit of the Senate seat, Speaker Patrick and President Offutt became the face(s) of Frankfort leadership. They were miles apart on most policy issues, but they made every effort possible to play well in the sandbox on matters of significant importance, namely BR 171 pre-filed by Patrick, which would repeal right-to-work legislation.

Despite baiting by the media, and some of his own members, President Offutt would not criticize Patrick, the bill, or its supporters. That should have been a clue to any decent political reporter, but given cutbacks and budget constraints in the media, decent reporters were a relic found on the pages of a political history book. Stuart Carroll penned a column that pointed out the incongruity of the bill and leadership's position on it, hinting that something more sinister was in play. No one paid attention. Stuart didn't have the following of famed journalists who had preceded him in the political press corps — names like Sy Ramsey, Ed Ryan, John Ed Pearce, Dick Wilson, Mark Chellgren, Ferrell Wellman, and even Tom Loftus.

He did have a following among FBI agents, particularly Rachel Whitney.

"Stuart, what the hell did I just read?" She posed the question to him on a burner phone he had provided.

"Agent Whitney, I have no idea what you're…"

"Bullshit, Stuart. Are you trying to sabotage our investigation?"

"I don't understand." He did, but wanted to become more involved rather than being at arm's length away from Whitney and her team. "I just reported the facts of the bill."

"That's crap and you know it, Stuart. Anyone with half a brain can read between the lines and know that there is more to the story than a simple bill filing. You're inviting a media armada to join you in exposing the situation and our role in it."

"But Agent Whitney, I don't know what…"

"Stuart, you have heard it before and you'll no doubt here it in the future because you are you. Shut the fuck up!"

There was a deafening silence on the phone.

An interminable amount of time passed, or seemed to. Whitney maintained silence on her end of the conversation. Stuart broke the awkward void.

"Agent Whitney, I'm sorry. I was completely out of line. I know that, and I know I will not repeat my mistake in the future. You told me to trust you, and I have. Now you need to trust me. We both want the same outcome. I can help you get there. I know you can help me."

"Stuart, there is nothing I would like to see more than Tony Barrows behind bars. If you can help me accomplish that, you will be rewarded. Again, I give you my word. But if you step in front of me on in front of this investigation like you did in this column, I will crush you. You understand?"

Stuart nodded, which offered Rachel little comfort since she couldn't see him. She shattered the silence.

"DO YOU UNDERSTAND ME?"

Stuart responded with a mousy "yes."

"Enough said, Mr. Carroll. Let's get about our work."

Stuart was all for that, or at least something other than the harpy screech of Agent Whitney.

"I'll be back in touch soon, Stuart. In the meantime, concentrate on compiling your background information. Based on what I've heard, you have enough work to keep you busy for quite a while."

He knew it. Rachel Whitney was the nameless voice on the phone call. The mere fact that she made a second effort to engage him with the material meant there was something in there — something he had missed in his initial review. He would not miss it again!

Chapter 36 — November

Fortunately for Kentuckians, this was an off year for elections. Nothing at all on the ballot, a saving grace enacted a few years back to give voters a break from incessant television, radio, and online commercials that drowned out everything around them. But November was not without its intrigue.

After weeks of digging, cajoling, and bribing certain Pikeville medical personnel, Stuart was finally able to write a story about Jack Adams' near-fatal foibles. He wasn't Tony Barrows, obviously, but he was close enough to Stuart's arch enemy that Tony got a mention in the story. The headline appeared two weeks before Thanksgiving.

Prominent Frankfort Lobbyist Defies Overdose Death

The subhead was even more damning for Tony.

Barrows and Adams Partner Saved at Pikeville Hospital

The rest of the story was even uglier than the headline. Stuart recounted the entire incident from the time Jack downed Oxycontin with a bourbon chaser in the trailer of his "girlfriend for the night." She panicked and called 9-1-1. Because it was a county ambulance run, certain information was available as public record despite federal HIPPA regulations. The balance was obtained with a money order mailed to each of the paramedics, who were among a number of anonymous sources cited in Stuarts's article.

Some of the others included the ER nurses who attended to Jack when his heart took a timeout. There was the doctor on call in the ER—an effort to legitimize his own practice so that his "pain clinic" would be more socially acceptable. And there was the orderly who wheeled Jack from the ER into a private room on the fifth floor—where Clement Combs waited for his grandson.

Stuart had it all in his story. Drugs, sex, political heavyweights, and more importantly to him, a direct link to Tony Barrows. The latter gave him opportunity to report on Tony's business, his relationship with Jack, his clients, and his reputation in the halls of the capitol, including quotes from some legislators who were no fans of Tony or Jack.

That afternoon edition of the *Frankfort State Journal* set the tone for events that would follow. Tony didn't like it at all. Jack was too hopped up with his newest girlfriend to understand. For his part, Stuart got a big "atta boy" from his editor and delighted in the fact that other newspapers and wire services were picking up the story.

Rachel Whitney and Tamara Looney were miles apart, but as they raised their cups of coffee in sync, you could almost hear the dull thud of stoneware and a toast—good government starts today.

Chapter 37 — It's a marathon, not a sprint

When Jack had been discharged from the hospital, Clement gave him two choices: rehab or rehab. In their first meeting after the near fatal night, Clement reached into his jacket pocket and threw a piece of paper at Jack.

"Pick your state and say goodbye to your 'friends' for six weeks. You're leaving right after Thanksgiving."

Clement stood silently while Jack was looking over the document—a single sheet formatted in a nice table listing all of the in-patient rehab facilities Clement's assistant had found for him. The old man was serious.

Jack tried to argue, but the Clement would have none of it. "You *will* get treatment in a rehab center and you will get your act cleaned up."

Well, Jack thought to himself, if he had to do rehab, then he could work on his tan over the winter months at a facility in Naples. Of course, Sun Tan City would be less expensive, but he needed to stay in the good graces of his grandfather. Six weeks in a Florida rehab center would get him through the awkward moments at Christmas when his mother always insisted on reading aloud the Matthew *and* Luke versions of the Virgin Birth. He would miss bowl season with his buds, and his Bud—but small sacrifice in order to keep Clement happy.

He managed to stay clean, which meant out of the hospital, through Thanksgiving. Clement was none the wiser, but Jack fell back into his pattern.

He commuted from Pikeville to Frankfort on Tuesdays and returned on Fridays to make sure he and Tony had client issues under control. The commute started with Kahlua and coffee from Tommy Goodrich at the local Speedway. Jack poured the coffee, and Tommy poured a generous does of the liqueur from a bottle Jack had provided.

While in Frankfort and away from Clement's prying eyes, it was business as usual. Bloody Mary for breakfast, vodka and tonic at lunch, premium bourbon of the day during happy hour, and a pill or two just to take off the edge while he nursed his final bourbon at the end of the day. Next day, it started again. His own version of lather, rinse, repeat.

On Thanksgiving Day—the day before he headed to Naples, he masked his early morning adventure with Lortab as a byproduct of the tryptophan in his mother's basted turkey. He was jarred out of his poultry induced coma by his grandfather, who was angered more than Jack had ever seen—veins pulsing, face reddening, breathing growing deeper and louder.

"What the hell is this?"

Stuart Carroll strikes again.

East Kentucky Power Broker Tied to KKK

The headline screamed at Clement and he screamed at Jack.

"These are your people, Jack. You have to stop this bullshit."

"Kinda hard to do from a Florida rehab center."

Peavler was mentioned. Jack was mentioned. Clement was center stage—and he was not happy.

"I don't give a rat's ass about your rehab date. Fix this and fix it now."

The old man's phone rang. Caller ID said it was Peavler.

"Fucking great. You get on the phone and fix this now. I'm going to try and get the dumbass Peavler off the ledge."

He moved slowly to a corner of the room where he spoke to the Senator in hushed tones.

"Peavler doesn't like seeing his name in the paper. So far, he has gotten calls from this Stuart character, reporters from the *Courier* and *Herald,* all but one of the TV stations in Louisville and Lexington, the one in Hazard since it's close to Hindman, and, friggin' Rachel Maddow's producer and Samantha Bee's staff!"

Jack tried cracking a joke about P.T. Barnum and publicity. It didn't work. Clement was in no mood to be entertained.

Clement leaned down and grabbed Jack by the shirt. He yanked so hard, that his grip slipped and he punched himself in the face. Jack tried to stifle a laugh. It didn't work. With that, Clement swung an open hand at Jack and struck him so hard that his gnarled fingers left a bright red imprint on Jack's unshaven face.

"Listen you little shit. I made you. I can break you just like I did that son-of-a-bitch that sired you. Don't test me, boy. Don't test me."

"Sorry, Granddaddy."

"I need Peavler for some work we need to get done in the next session. I need you to ride herd on it, but I need you healthy, sober and with a clear head. Rehab is the only way to make sure you don't screw things up!"

"What are you talking about. I don't know anything about Peavler and legislation you need."

"It has to do with energy, you idiot. What else do you think I want?"

"How? What?"

"We're flying under the radar right now, son. But when the time is right, Peavler is going to ask for a special tariff on natural gas that is burned in power plants. Gas is killing us because it's so damned cheap. The tariff will subsidize coal production to make it more competitive with gas. But the best part is that a generous chunk of the tariff will go toward energy exploration and alternative sources for generating electricity."

"But won't that just help the tree huggers," Jack asked with a naivety that Clement couldn't understand. He finally managed to laugh for the first time since he walked into the room.

"Jack, sometimes you're a dumbass. That energy exploration fund will go to companies that have been hurt by the coal bust so that they can put more miners back to work. It starts with a pilot research project conducted by Yellow Creek Energy."

"Granddaddy, you sly sumbitch."

"Think about it, Jackie. Utilities generate 8.3 million megawatt hours of electricity from gas. That's 8.3 *billion* kilowatt hours. Peavler's bill will put half a penny for each kWh into the research fund—our research fund. Do the math, son. That's $41.5 million in the first year alone and we don't have to lift a finger. But this KKK shit could bring it all down."

"Chances of passing?"

"Slim and none if you keep pissing off Peavler and if you don't get your head screwed on straight. Now you get on the phone and get this shit stopped."

His call went, of course, to Tony. He was as incensed as Clement.

"Jack, this is not good. Not good at all. Peavler is compromised and that puts us, and Riley, in a dangerous spot. This is the FBI. I know it is. Somehow, they have gotten wind of what we're doing, and they want to derail us before we get started."

"I say, 'fuck 'em all.' This is what happens. The press latches on to granddad and Peavler. While they're both trying to fend off the media attack, we go about our merry way with Offutt and Patrick. They're the ones we give a shit about. The fibbees are actually doing us a favor by distracting things around Peavler."

There was an uneasy quiet on the phone while Tony processed Jack's theory.

"Makes sense," he finally said. "Can we get together next week to run through all of the eventualities?"

"Sorry, bro. Headed out for six weeks in the Naples sun to go through rehab for granddaddy. I'll be back before the filing deadline in January. We all know that nothing happens in Frankfort until that deadline passes.

"I'll basically be without any contact to the real world. Give your wife a kiss for me, and her friend, Bridget. We'll all have some fun on the other side of this rehab shit."

Clement accompanied Jack to Naples, into the rehab center, and through his entrance questionnaire.

"Drug of choice?"

Vodka, bourbon, tequila, Oxy, blow, a little Xanax, Lortab, pretty much anything that was on the market. He was unapologetic for anything he said.

His bags were searched for drugs and alcohol. Clement tried to assure the registration nurse that Jack was clean and working to stay clean. She mumbled a "thank you, Mr. Clements," a she removed two vials of something along with a 90-day supply of pain medicine from an obscure pocket in Jack's bag.

Once Clement knew that Jack was settled in, he took a cab to his condo on the Gulf in Old Naples. He had phoned ahead to make sure the place was ready for his arrival. As the elevator doors opened, he saw a table of fresh shrimp, cheeses, antipasto, a variety of breads, a selection of wines, and a bar that had a tumbler of ice and bourbon waiting for him. He also saw Hannah, the housekeeper, lounging on the lanai wearing the only thing God had given her at birth. Her silky brown skin glistened in the rays of sun as it descended into the western sky.

Clement took a long drink of the bourbon. When he set the glass back down on the bar, Hannah turned, "Mr. Combs, you startled me."

He poured himself another three fingers of Eagle Rare.

"Hannah, my dear, I am in a foul mood. My grandson is hurting me on a number of fronts. Do you think you could ease my pain?"

"Why, Mr. Combs, I am so sorry. You know I will do everything I can to ease your pain."

With that, she raised her nubile body from the chaise and moved toward Clement.

She tiptoed to kiss the old man. He returned the favor and let his hands wander over the milk chocolate that defined her body. They retreated to the bedroom in perfect timing with his Viagra.

He was a racist; he wasn't stupid. Hannah would be his for the weekend, and he would like nothing better.

The weekend would be busy for Rachel Whitney as well. She had kept tabs on Jack since he was discharged from the hospital. It's amazing how cooperative federal judges can be on wiretaps when political corruption is the end game.

She listened to him at home, in his car, even at Speedway where Tommy Goodrich was earning his confidential informant merit badge. But nothing had prepared her for the little energy exploits Clement had confided to his grandson. Her investigation of government corruption had just been expanded. She had six weeks to put the pieces together before Jack came back to town and started working for his grandfather in addition to Tony and the labor guys.

She lifted the receiver on a secure landline and dialed the number Cary O'Brien had given her in Charlotte. She uttered six words that immediately got his attention.

"Director O'Brien, we need more troops."

Chapter 38 — Hey, it's good to be back home again

December flew by for everyone, as it normally does. The few weeks between Thanksgiving and Christmas allow most folks, including politicians, to take it easy and enjoy fellowship with friends and family.

Those weeks were a blur for Tony, Tamara, Rachel, Stuart, Clement, and the entire cast of unholy characters, but not because of fellowship. Quite the contrary. Tempers flared. Strategies were developed, scrapped, redeveloped, and scrapped again.

It was a little different for Jack. His clock was moving ever so slowly as he 'enjoyed' seven days in detox, followed by meeting after meeting with doctors, psychiatrists, counselors, behavioral psychologists, and his 12-step posse.

Finally, January 6. His rehab had been completed. He would be headed home and back into the loving arms of whoever would have him. The six-week hiatus had allowed him to reflect on a number of things: his work, his grandfather, his friends, his real purpose in life, and where he could score some coke for his welcome home party. More than half of all addicts will relapse at some point. Jack was a leader on that statistical curve, as he proved over a vodka martini in the airport lounge awaiting his flight to Lexington.

January 9, he was back in Frankfort with Tony in the capitol annex as they had been so many times before. Mary Beth was there. Bridget, who had left the law firm to join Tony as an administrative assistant, was also there. Jack wanted an edge to get back on the job, so he was wired with cocaine and caffeine. Bridget was simply wired — the type that allowed Rachel to listen in on their every word.

The banter started as soon as everyone sat at the table.

"Jack, my boy. You're looking great! Good to have you back, man. Good to have you back."

"So where are we, Tony? I've been out of the loop for six weeks! The only work I have done has been to fraternize with a couple of nurses when no one was looking."

Tony let out one of his boisterous laughs.

"Leave it to you to find tail even in rehab. Next time, you may want to check in for sex addiction."

Mary Beth and Bridget shifted uneasily in their chairs. Tony's laugh drew attention from half the people in the cafeteria.

"Here's where we are, Jack. Patrick is going to drop his bill on February 26 — last day to file legislation in the House. Leadership is going to put it on hold until later. We only need five days to pass both chambers, send it to a conference committee and on to Lyons' desk. Meanwhile. Shaughnessy is stoking the labor guys to have a presence in the annex on a daily basis — slow at first with a steady increase in numbers until we have a few thousand union supporters roaming the halls. Stengel is churning his PR machine with ads on TV and radio, that will be reinforced with calls and direct mail closer to Patrick dropping the bill.

"And here's the beautiful thing. Thanks to old Clement, we have Peavler on our side in the Senate. I had a little conversation with him and politely suggested that the only way in hell his little energy shell game would pass was if I got our guys to back it. Last month, Clement wouldn't give me the time of day. Now, it's like I'm a second grandson — his favorite grandson."

That stung a little at first. But then Jack decided he didn't really give a shit as long as he was in the old man's will.

"So, we cool our jets until the mid-March, make sure nobody goes off the reservation, and then it's full speed ahead. By the time we reach *sine die*, opponents won't know what hit them."

"Let me get this straight," Jack finally spoke. "We pass Patrick's bill in the House that completely repeals right-to-work. The Senate amends it enough that it has to go before a conference committee. When it gets to conference, the compromise is a hybrid bill passing that requires workers in a union shop to donate what would be their dues to a special fund in support of spouses and children of union members who were hurt or killed on the job. And we get a part of the 75 cents the union takes on every dollar going into the fund?"

"Bingo, Jack my boy. This will be the easiest money I've made since Mrs. Walker's cat!"

Of course, no one knew what Tony was talking about, but they knew they would soon be splitting a boatload of cash with more to come in the future.

"I say we head to Seraphini's to celebrate," Jack was excited to be back in his favorite haunt and equally excited about spending the afternoon with two lovely ladies and his best friend.

"Didn't you just get out of rehab," asked a confused Bridget.

"No, I just spent $40,000 of granddaddy's money to get a good tan. Drinks are on me."

Chapter 39 — March Madness begins

Weeks passed since Jack's auspicious homecoming. The legislature trudged along, approving pissant resolutions and a few, inconsequential laws, but nothing on the order of what was about to happen.

(Oh, in the real March Madness — the NCAA basketball championship — Kentucky didn't make the tourney after a dismal 16 and 18 season. It may have been a foreshadowing of more losses in the state, as in loss of freedom.)

Finally, the big day arrived. Showtime. Patrick was ready to take the stage. He got a little pep talk from Tony in the hall, who motioned to his right. Across the way stood Melissa and Melanie — Patrick's old friends from the golf course.

Tony bent down to whisper in Patrick's ear, "the girls really like powerful and successful men. If this bill starts taking flight today, I'm sure they would help you celebrate the first step."

They weren't in Daisy Dukes or halter tops. They actually looked like they were lobbyists working the legislators. Of course, it's true that their dresses were a little too tight and little too short. But there were lots of women who could fit that bill — lobbyists, staffers, visitors, and even a couple of middle-aged legislators trying to recapture their youth. The M&M girls blended right in.

Patrick felt himself reacting to the two lovelies that stood across from him next to the committee room door. As he turned to enter, Tony gave him a slap on the back and said, "go get 'em Mr. Speaker."

He stood a little more erect in a couple of places and marched to the door with head held high. When he passed Melissa and Melanie, they both gave him a little pat, too, only it wasn't on the back and it lasted a little longer as the Speaker waited for the doorway to clear. The girls were shielded from sight because of the angle as they faced Patrick. Melanie stroked and spoke, "why Mr. Speaker, I do believe I left something in your office while running errands for Tony. When you finish, do you think Melissa and I could follow you to look for the package."

She winked, but it was totally unnecessary. He knew what he was going to do as soon as she opened her mouth.

"Ladies, I'll see you in my office in about 30 minutes."

That will give him ample time to offer his testimony and get the Viagra working in his system.

"I won't give up until we find the package, no ma'am, won't give up."

And they say chivalry is dead.

The girls offered a final pat on the pants, headed to Patrick's office to 'get more comfortable,' and watch the whole thing on closed circuit TV.

As they passed Tony, Melissa mouthed 'you owe us big time' and held up four fingers followed by an unsaid 'each.'

Tony laughed aloud but nodded his approval of the demand.

A gavel came down hard with Labor Chairman Bill Kerr attached to the other end.

"This is the regular meeting of the House Labor and Industry Committee. The clerk will take the roll."

A few mundane moments passed as the LRC staff member charged with attendance gold stars did her roll call. Not a full house, but enough for a quorum. Maybe a few more will show.

"We're pleased to have with us today, Speaker Theodore Patrick to address his bill, HB 417. This is an important piece of legislation for the Commonwealth. Mr. Speaker, welcome. You may proceed."

Patrick was setting down a glass of water he had used for the little blue pill.

"Thank you, Mr. Chairman, ladies and gentlemen of the committee, and to my own staff that has worked so diligently on this bill. House Bill 417 is a repeal of right-to-work legislation, which has targeted the middle class for extinction."

He was interrupted by Doug Kolaski, an old-timer from Harlan, "Mr. Chairman, I move for passage of HB 417."

"Second," came from the other side of the dais where Phil Bern examined fingernails to see if a manicure would be in order.

Kerr resumed, "We have a motion to accept HB 417 as presented by its sponsor. All in favor?"

Some weak 'ayes' could be heard among members.

"Opposed?"

Crickets.

"The ayes have it. HB 417 is passed favorably, and since there was no expressed opposition, we could put it..."

Kolaski interrupted, "Motion, Mr. Chairman, to put HB 417 on the consent calendar."

"We have a motion..."

"Second," this time from Judy Lake, seated next to Kolaski

"Without objection, House Bill 417 is to be placed on the consent calendar for action by the full body. There being no other business to come before the committee, we stand adjourned. Thank you, Speaker Patrick."

Kerr offered a nod and a wink to Patrick, but he was really looking over the Speaker's shoulder at Amber, who was now seated next to Tony. Amber just smiled knowing that the afternoon would be theirs and likely at 1PP.

Tony leaped to his feet and immediately started making calls on his cell phone. Ramming pet legislation through a committee is not without precedence. It has happened many times, but this was special for Tony and he was grinning widely as he chatted with Riley, Stengel and Flannery. All were pleased.

Bridget and Mary Beth had watched the hearing from the LRC employee's lounge. They offered a high five, and after a quick glance to make sure they were alone, they exchanged a quick kiss followed by another high five.

Jack was down the street hanging out with another lobbyist friend. He had a suite of offices, a big screen to watch the action, and an open bar that Jack enjoyed to its fullest. He raised his glass of Knob Creek and motioned to the television, "we're on our way, Tony. On our way."

Outside the committee room, Teddy Patrick dodged a pack of reporters shouting questions that went unanswered. His overarching concern had little to do with the media, the legislation, or even the strategy for next steps. No, he was fretting that the committee meeting happened so quickly, the Viagra won't have kicked in when he sees Melanie and Melissa.

He still made a beeline for his office.

In the wake of the committee's action sat a number of Chamber of Commerce types all talking at the same time to each other. All blaming someone else for not knowing about this snowball rolling down the hill. All pledging to kill the bill when it got to the Senate. They firmly believed that had the troops, the message, and the political wherewithal to bring the legislation to a quick and painful death. Some people also believe in Santa Claus. He would have about as much influence in stopping this runaway train as the Chamber guys did.

Chapter 40 — And now the Ides of March

During legislative sessions, most state houses are like a three-ring circus, complete with jugglers, tightrope walkers, sideshow freaks, and — of course — clowns. Frankfort is no exception, although one could argue that it has a disproportionate number of freaks and clowns, all of which were about to be on display in the center ring.

HB 417 breezed through the full House as part of the consent agenda, which means nobody really had to explain anything except to say 'aye' in a voice vote.

Now, it was on to the Senate Labor and Industry Committee, which was not nearly as friendly to Tony and his client as Rep. Kerr was in the House. Darren Peavler did his part to assure safe passage in the Senate, but he needed Tony's help in the House.

Peavler's little energy bill had cleared the upper chamber easily and was now in the Democratically controlled House. The Energy Committee was loaded with coal supporters from Eastern and Western Kentucky, but the Chairman was a tree-hugging, limousine liberal from Louisville, who just happened to be Speaker Patrick's son-in-law — Brent Spencer. Whenever he managed to remove the silver spoon from this mouth, it was usually to tout wind or solar as the future of energy production in Kentucky. On more than one occasion, he would say, "Coal and gas are as dead as the dinosaurs that created them."

Peavler needed Tony and Jack to get the bill heard in committee. There were enough coal guys on both sides of the aisle to pass it, but the little prick from Prospect stood in the way. This is where the jugglers took center stage.

Tony had convinced Speaker Patrick to have the energy bill on the committee agenda, or more specifically, Melissa and Melanie had convinced him. SIL Spencer didn't want to piss off the Speaker and his wife's dear daddy, so he agreed. In the back of his mind, though, he was going to use discussion of the bill to expound the evils of fossil fuels.

Funny how things work out.

On the morning of the committee meeting, Spencer got a call from Teddy, who said that there was a family emergency in Louisville and they both needed to get there right away. Something happened to Brent's son, Brent III, more commonly known as Trey. Patrick and Spencer met in the parking garage and sped toward the Interstate for the 45-minute drive to Norton's Children's Hospital.

It was *en route* that Spencer finally started to ask himself questions after the initial panic subsided. Why did Teddy get the call and not him? Who called? His wife or his mother-in-law? What sort of emergency? Why the hospital? Wasn't Trey supposed to be in preschool?

When they were within rock throwing distance of the hospital, Teddy's phone rang—his wife. He put it on the car speaker.

"Honey, how's Trey?"

"He's better now. Had a bit of a coughing fit at preschool, so I brought him to the ER. The school called me because they couldn't reach Olivia. She was in a yoga class and couldn't hear the phone ring."

"Do we need to come on? Brent is with me."

"No, sweetheart, I think we're good. Trey is resting, and Olivia is on her way."

"You're sure."

"Yes, Teddy. You and Brent go back and do the people's business. Trey will be fine."

Brent Spencer had just been played by his crafty father-in-law. Since the legislative session was winding down, it was imperative that committees start clearing their dockets of any bills that had a snowball's chance in hell of passing—as was the case with HB 417. In Chairman Spencer's absence, David Tarter took over as vice-chairman. Peavler's bill went through in a split decision—coalfield guys 6, urban liberals 3. The energy legislation that was so dear to Clement Combs was on its way to the full House.

In the halls outside the meeting room, Jack approached Senator Peavler.

"Congratulations, Darren. You got yours, now we need your help to get ours."

Peavler nodded but said nothing. He was off to his office to start making phone calls—to key members of the House drumming up support for his bill, and a long conversation with the Senate Labor and Industry chairman about HB 417. It had to have a hearing, and it had to pass. He didn't need a home run like the bill got in the House, but it needed to be a solid double, which put it within scoring distance on the Senate floor.

Darren Peavler used lots of sports analogies in his conversations. Some people understood; some didn't.

Fortunately, the Senate Labor and Industry chair was a former pro baseball player who spent three seasons with the Reds before his propensity for the high life with wine and women started eating into his already anemic batting average. Rather than go back to the minors, he decided to work for the family business, which was buying and selling political favors.

"Anything for a friend for a fee," he laughed. "I understand. Do you understand, Darren?"

Peavler was perfectly quiet on his end.

"Do you understand, Darren?"

Peavler was thinking to himself that rumors of an FBI presence in Frankfort had circulated annually since the old BOPTROT sting. What if the rumors were true this year? Would a simple "yes" get him in trouble. He would have to take his chances or be exposed for his Klan activities.

"I understand," he finally said.

"And we understand," said Special Agent Joe Rider — one of the new troops brought on to help out Agent Whitney and her gang of feds.

Chapter 41 — Gang's All Here

The clock was winding down for the General Assembly session. For the first time in years, the legislature actually approved a budget that didn't have to go to a conference committee. When you have shrinking revenue, it's easy to come to consensus on a spending plan. Keep the lights of state government on, and that's about it.

A proposed tax increase died a loud and miserable death when two lawmakers on opposite sides of the issue came to physical blows on the floor of the House.

The pension system for state employees and teachers kept spiraling out of control with the amount of unfunded liability increasing with every day.

But there was important legislation passed, like designating the Eastern hellbender salamander as the official state amphibian. Another example of good government at work.

Two critical and somewhat controversial bills remained — Peavler's SB 44, which was headed for the full House, and HB 417 on its way to the full Senate.

Interestingly, ironically, coincidentally, or connivingly, both were placed on the Orders of the Day March 21, leaving only four days before a two-week break that reconvened for the final two days of the session. If both passed, they would be assigned to a conference committee because of minor differences between House and Senate versions. That's exactly what Tony and his troops wanted; Peavler and Clement were less favorable toward a conference committee, but were forced to accept the cards that were dealt them.

On the night of March 19, planning meetings abounded.

Tony had his cast of misfit boys out to 1 PP for dinner, drinks, and strategy development. All of the major players were there: Riley Shaughnessy, Teddy Patrick, Larry Offutt, Jimmy Flannery, Fred Stengel, Bill Kerr (with Amber on his arm), Mary Beth with Bridget (of course), and Governor Lyons even joined by Skype from his Senate campaigning in Western Kentucky. The Bosnian cleaning ladies who doubled as Tony's personal Hooters' girls provided a succulent dinner and made sure no one's glass was ever empty.

In Naples, Clement leered at Hannah, who was busying herself prepping for a different meeting—one that involved only Darren Peavler and Jack. They would fly in on Combs' private plane, and spend the evening developing contingencies on virtually any situation that could surface in the House or in conference.

And in the Shelbyville hotel meeting room where Rachel Whitney had practically lived for the past eight months, was an equally impressive group of A-listers, including Lieutenant Governor Looney, Stan Duncan, and Karen Wilson from the U.S. Attorney's office, and Attorney General Robert Breckinridge. Rachel's team of FBI investigators surrounded the inner circle seated at the conference table. In the corner like a fly on the wall was Stuart Carroll. Just as Agent Whitney had promised, he would get his exclusive and it started now.

At 1 PP, Tony roared loudly above the din of his homeboy Babel to get everyone's attention.

"Tonight, we lay out a plan, tomorrow we gather our troops, and in two days, we carry this piece of history to victory. But an army marches on its stomach, so let us give thanks to the lovely ladies who prepared this meal for us, give thanks to the men and women who have supported our efforts, and give thanks that we're all going to be filthy rich in a few days."

With that, he raised his glass of Pappy Van Winkle and toasted his comrades in arms.

At the Naples condo, where Clement was spending more and more time away from Pikeville and with Hannah, he offered a toast as well.

"There are two things that have made America great. Straight talk and crooked politicians. Here's to both who have served us and our causes well."

Peavler was a little uneasy toasting with a black woman straddling Clement's lap. He was a racist and he was stupid. Clement didn't care.

Jack lifted the glass of sweet tea he had been served to appease his grandfather. Hannah, however, had made sure there was bourbon in his bedroom, and after Clement wore out and drifted off, she would show Jack where it was hidden, and so much more.

In the Shelbyville conference room, stale coffee and bad pizza were the sustenance to keep the white hats alive. Rachel Whitney dominated the conversation with her instructions. Even district director Carey O'Brien, who had flown in from Charlotte for the fun, was spellbound at how poised, professional, and passionate she was with what the next steps would be.

"This is the way it will go down tomorrow. Word will leak — Stuart, do you have that — that a grand jury has handed up indictments, sealed indictments so no one will know whose ox will be gored. That will appear in the *State Journal* tomorrow afternoon. Tomorrow night, we're going to have a press conference at the federal building where the 'attorneys' will take center stage, including you, Governor Looney. On Tuesday, our guys along with state police and KBI agents will start the roundup, which will include a presence to arrest those indicted on the House and Senate floors, as well as in the Governor's office.

"This is going to shine a beacon of light on political corruption that will sweep across the country. Kentucky is ground-zero in the war on graft. We have other task forces in Louisiana, Mississippi, Michigan, Georgia, Illinois, and Alabama gathering similar information on legislators. But it all starts with us.

"I want to thank each and every one of you in this room for your diligence, thoroughness, and patience in dealing with this investigation."

She capped off her pep talk with the same line she had used when she and Tamara Looney first met, "We know that there is an underbelly in our society bent on taking down our institutions and we want to do everything we can to stop it."

The Lieutenant Governor echoed with an emphatic, "Amen."

Attorney General Breckinridge took his turn at rallying the troops.

"The most important thing we have to do is preempt passage of SB 22 and HB 417. If we allow these bills to pass and go to a conference committee, nothing will be able to derail the train: no arrests, no indictments, no investigation will technically prevent them from becoming law. We can't afford to have these issues tied up in court for a single minute. Given how Frankfort works, a sympathetic judge could allow the bills to become law while appeals play out. This is bad legislation sponsored by bad men, and it needs to be aborted immediately."

"Don't worry, Rob," said Governor Looney. "If Damien goes down and is arrested, I become the Governor and I still have a few days to execute a veto. We're all good. But you're right. We should make every effort to abort this sleazy crap as soon as possible."

After two more hours of logistics discussion, the feds all retired to their rooms. Stuart went back to Frankfort to start filing his story. Rachel and Tamara were left in the conference room alone.

"A word, Agent Whitney."

"Yes, ma'am."

"When Damien goes down, I become the Governor. As such, I get to appoint a Lieutenant Governor."

"Yes, ma'am."

"I have been impressed with you ever since your operation in Atlanta. I would like for you to consider becoming my LG."

"Oh, Governor Looney, I'm flattered," she paused before offering a polite, but adamant response. "I'm a cop; always have been, always will be. I'm not a politician. My dad always told me to follow my passion, and that means bringing down bad guys who prey on those who don't have anyone to be their champion. As I said, I am flattered by the offer, but I'm a cop and want to stay where I think I can do the most good."

"I respect that, Rachel. But if you change your mind, you have first right of refusal. Now let's get this thing done and put these assholes away."

Clement was down for the count before he even got it up. The Ambien that Hannah had substituted in his drink instead of the Viagra did exactly what she wanted. Peavler took a cab back to the airport for a late-night return to Kentucky so he would be in the Capitol the next day to tie up any loose ends on SB 44. Jack had retired to his room and sank deep into the spa tub when Hannah walked in with two glasses, a bottle of bourbon, and a smile.

Uber sent a fleet of drivers to 1 PP to pick up all of the drunk celebrants. Chairman Kerr stayed in a guest room with Amber. Tony peeled off a couple of the maids for his nightly entertainment. Bridget and Mary Beth went to their room for another night together — or perhaps, the last as Bridget thought about what was going to happen in the next 48 hours. She started weeping, which surprised Mary Beth.

"Is something wrong? Is there something I did?"

"No, Mary Beth. I'm fine. Just hold me; hold me all night. I love you."

MB offered nothing but a hug and a long, passionate kiss. They fell asleep in each other's arms as they had done so many years ago in Gulf Shores. Bridget thought to herself that she wished this moment could last forever. But she knew that what was about to happen would make that difficult at best, and more probably, impossible.

Chapter 42 — The quiet before the storm

By population, Frankfort is the fourth smallest state capital in the U.S. By appearance, it has to be in the bottom 10 in terms of ugliness. By political corruption, it ranks at or near the top, which is of little solace to anyone other than those on the take. The entire state, as well as many political observers at the national level, was about to get a civics lesson.

Peavler picked up a burner phone at an airport kiosk and started making calls. First to those in the House who could help his (and Clement's) energy bill. And then to his colleagues in the Senate who could shepherd passage of the repeal of Right to Work — HB 417.

In the midst of his coalition building, he got a call on the burner, but that was impossible. He hadn't given the number out to anyone. He didn't recognize the number that was calling. He was completely dumbfounded. But rather than let it go to voicemail, he answered, an act he would regret for the rest of his life.

"Hello?"

"Senator Peavler. This is FBI Special Agent Rachel Whitney. Don't hang up, sir, we have to meet with you as soon as possible. Please clear your calendar and meet us at the address I am about to text to you. 8:00 a.m. sharp. Do you have any questions?"

A joke? Someone on his staff pulling a prank? But how did they get the number? How did anyone know about the burner?

His phone pinged with an address. 3480 Brownsboro Road in Louisville. He knew that address, but couldn't remember why.

He mustered all of the bravado he could.

"Do you know who you are talking to? Do you know how much power I have in the legislature?"

Rachel shut him down.

"Yes, Senator, I know exactly who you are. I know who Tony Barrows is. I know who Clement Combs is. I know who Jack Adams is. And frankly, I don't give a rat's ass. I also know who the Grand Dragon is for the KKK in Southeastern Kentucky. You have any other questions?"

He fell silent. His bravado was reduced to that of a whimpering puppy. And then it hit him. 3480 Brownsboro Road was the home of Lt. Governor Tamara Looney. He had paid his respects there after the funeral for her husband. But why Tamara's house and why the FBI?

Why indeed?

His sleep was fitful. The alarm was set, but never used because he woke well in advance of his Barbra Streisand wake-up call. He was on the road by 7:00. Plenty of time to make it to the Brownsboro Road address even with rush hour traffic.

When he arrived, he was greeted by Tamara Looney with Bloody Mary in hand.

"Here Darren, you're going to need this."

Still confused, he walked into the home where his friend and part-time lover, Dave Tunie, had resided. He gingerly sipped the Bloody Mary. For all he knew it was laced with something that would make him regret having ever been there. The drink wasn't spiked, but he regretted it nonetheless.

Chapter 43 — The tapestry starts to unravel

"Darren, let me introduce you. This is Special Agent Rachel Whitney with the FBI. And this is District Director Cary O'Brien from the Charlotte office. You know General Breckinridge. And these are the U.S. Attorneys from the Eastern and Western Districts of Kentucky, Stan Duncan and Karen Wilson."

"Tamara, why am I here and what are they doing here?"

"Senator Peavler, in parlance that you may understand, your ass is ours," said Rachel. "We have you on vote buying, selling your influence for the purpose of defrauding the state, and if you'd like to push it, we could add a hate crime charge because of your leadership in the Klan and its activities of late to threaten and injure African Americans in Eastern Kentucky.

"You're going down, sir. It's up to you as to how far."

Tamara interrupted, "And don't forget, Darren, your relationship with Dave. I found it in his diary after he killed himself. I'm not sure your Klan buddies would like the fact that their grand poohbah is gay. That would be a far worse punishment than going to a federal Club Med."

"So, what do you want," the words barely audible as Peavler abandoned any measure of being a power broker.

"We want Clement Combs on a platter," said Duncan. "And we want your cooperation in our investigation of Tony Barrows and Jack Adams for their horse trading with your bill and HB 417."

"And if I decline your generous offer," the sarcasm was dripping.

"The indictment is ready to go. We have the wherewithal to fry your lily-white ass. The only question is whether you serve your time in a federal country club lockup, or in a maximum-security facility that makes Gitmo look like a day at the beach," Rachel was stern in her demeanor. Peavler was nonplused, or at least he was on the surface.

"I'll have to think about it. I'll talk it over with counsel and she'll be in touch. Tamara, thank you for the drink. I'll be on my way now."

The attorneys and investigators were bewildered by his attitude. As he slammed the door on his way out, they looked at each other in disbelief. What was he thinking? How could he turn down this deal?

Once he turned from Brownsboro Road onto the Gene Snyder Expressway, he started making phone calls. The first to his wife to say that he wouldn't be home until the weekend because of the frenetic pace of the legislature in the waning days of the session. The second was to his brother-in-law, who also was his insurance agent. He made sure all premiums were up to date on his life policy. The third was to Clement Combs. He knew that the FBI was probably listening to every call he made, but at this point, he didn't care.

"Clement, they know," that's all he said. There was silence on the other end of the call. He repeated himself, "Clement, they know. What are we supposed to do? Should you call Roscoe?"

Roscoe Bodine was a former Navy Seal who has washed out because of mental illness issues related prescription drug addiction. He was Clement's enforcer — the go to guy when Clement needed something fixed on a permanent basis.

"I'll take care of things," the only words that Clement spoke.

Peavler made one other call, to the House Majority Leader asking that SB 44 be pulled from the orders of the day. If he were going to leave a legacy, it would not be bad legislation that the courts would throw out anyway.

The Grey Goose poured freely for Peavler when he reached his Frankfort apartment. The sips of Bloody Mary at Tamara's house had whetted his appetite. It was 11:00 in the morning, but Peavler was well on his way to an unhealthy buzz. He would spend no time on capitol hill this day. Instead, he ordered lunch from Seraphini's. Normally, the restaurant doesn't deliver, but with someone of Darren Peavler's stature, exceptions could be made.

Fried oysters for an appetizer; wedge salad; hot brown for the entrée. He had paid for the meal by credit card, but wanted to tip the delivery boy. All he had on him was one Benjamin Franklin. He handed it over to the tattooed hand that was extended and uttered only two words, "Keep it."

The oysters were exquisite. The salad rather pedestrian, but what can you do with a wedge of iceberg. The hot brown was to die for. And as he finished his last bite, he did just that. Roscoe Bodine showed up at Peavler's apartment between the appetizer and salad. He sat patiently on the sofa while Peavler finished his meal. Peavler pushed the plate away. He sat perfectly still as Roscoe approached him from behind, leveled a .22 at the back of his head, and pulled the trigger. Peavler collapsed onto the table. Roscoe helped himself to three leftover oysters, and was then on his way.

There would be no country club imprisonment for Darren Peavler. He also avoided the hell of a gay, white supremacist in a maximum-security prison.

The energy bill was as dead as its sponsor. Clement would not be able to get his pet legislation passed — at least not in this General Assembly session. He would try again next year, he thought. The feds had a completely different thought in mind.

Chapter 44 — In like a lamb, out like a lion

Normally, the murder of someone of Darren Peavler's stature would dominate the headlines. But his body wasn't discovered until after the morning news cycle. And by the time the afternoon issue of the *State Journal* hit the streets, Peavler's death would be but a footnote on the FBI investigation and grand jury indictments.

True to her word, Rachel had provided Stuart Carroll with enough information to run with the story. No names were used because sources needed to remain anonymous and the indictments were sealed. The news spread as quickly as a brush fire up some dry and godforsaken canyon in California.

Every major news outlet in the country was calling trying to get information directly from Stuart. Most were sending crews of their own to Kentucky to catch up on the story. The airports in Lexington and Louisville were destinations for more private planes than at any time other than Derby or the Keeneland Select Yearling sale.

Tony was tipped to the story by a pressman he knew at the newspaper. He got a sense of what was coming, that essentially meant his entire world was crashing down around him.

He reached Jack, who was still at his grandfather's house in Naples. His only words were, "Get your ass home as quickly as you possibly can. We're sinking like a rock in quicksand."

Jack showered, shaved, and dressed in record time. He even turned down a most generous offer from Hannah for a repeat performance of last night's Restonic rumba. He sped to the airport in one of the cars Clement kept for personal use while in Florida.

Impatiently, he approached the ticket agent, "I need to get to Lexington as soon as possible. What do you have? It's an emergency."

"Which Lexington sir. Lexington, Virginia, Kentucky, or Lexington, Massachusetts? Interestingly, did you know there are 22 Lexingtons in the U.S. Lexington. The one in Mass is the oldest. Lexington, of course the site for the Revolutionary War had..."

Jack was even less patient now! He caught a glance of the agent's name badge and said, "Look, Gary, I don't give a fuck about how many Lexingtons there are. I need to get to the only Lexington that has a fucking airport near here. Lexington, Kentucky. How quickly can I get there?"

Delta ticket agent Gary Hall was totally dejected as he scanned the screen on his computer terminal.

"Here to Atlanta on Flight 227. Atlanta to Lexington on Flight 668. You'll arrive by 6:00. But it comes with a premium because the 14-day window has closed. You know, if you make reservations 14 days before a flight, the rates are less expensive."

"Gary, were you dropped on your fucking head as a child. I said I need to get to Lexington as soon as I can. I don't give a fuck about the cost or your fucking 14-day window. Get me on the fucking plane."

"Technically, sir, it's a jet, not a plane because..."

Poor Gary never finished the sentence. Jack leaned across the ticket counter with so much anger in his eyes that the ticket agent felt himself melting.

"I want you to issue me a fucking ticket now. I have no baggage to check. I have no carry on. I have enough cash to pay for the fucking ticket and I want it now!"

The agent worked as fast as he could to get boarding passes for Fort Myers to Atlanta and Atlanta to Lexington.

"Here you go, sir, and have a nice day."

Jack just shook his head, stormed toward the security check and the TSA scrutiny that would follow.

His phone rang again while he was waiting in line. Mary Beth this time.

"Jack, we're in deep trouble. I'm not sure what Tony told you, but the world is going to hell. This is going to be impossible for us to overcome if even half of what we're hearing on the hill is true. I have to go radio silent. I know we're bugged. I'll text you when I can. Get home quickly. Be safe."

Jack reached the security conveyer, dropped his phone, keys, and money clip in a funky gray plastic bowl. Removed his shoes and discovered that in his haste to get to the airport, he forgot to put on socks. Not a problem in Florida, but an early spring snow in Kentucky had the temperature sitting at 29. Of course, as fast as the blood and adrenaline were pumping through him, getting cold was the least of his worries.

Chapter 45 — Déjà vu all over again

It takes a little less than two hours to fly from Fort Myers to Atlanta. In that time, Jack consumed enough bourbon to start taking the edge off a bit. Maybe Tony and Mary Beth were exaggerating. Maybe the whole damned city was overreacting to a news story that would fade away. Maybe this tempest in a teapot would subside so that HB 417 could pass in the Senate? Maybe Santa Claus, the Easter Bunny, and Bigfoot would do a joint appearance on the Late Show with Stephen Colbert. It was just as likely.

Jack maneuvered his way through the concourses at Hartsfield-Jackson to the gate for Flight 668. Once he knew he was in the right spot and had a little time to kill, he took a seat at the bar located just down the way.

"What's your best bourbon," he asked.

The bartender didn't know he was about to set off a cultural war, "We get a lot of requests for Jack Daniels."

"Jack Daniels is a fucking Tennessee whiskey, not bourbon. What kind of bourbon do you have, dumbass?"

As Jack freaked out over the difference between the whiskies, he noticed the bartender's name tag. Garry. Different spelling, same dumbass.

"I see Makers on the shelf. Give me a double — neat."

"Ladies and gentlemen, we will begin boarding Flight 668 to Lexington in about 10 minutes..."

The rest of the announcement tailed off into nothingness as Jack stared at his iPhone hitting refresh on his email again and again waiting to hear from Mary Beth. The cheap suit sitting next to him had ordered Scotch, aka brandy. He offered to top off Jack's bourbon in hopes of engaging him in a deeper conversation. He knew they were both attorneys, from Kentucky, headed to Lexington, but that's about as much as he could drag out of Jack, who was and continued to be fixated on his phone. So, he resigned himself to nurse his Scotch/brandy alone all the while watching Jack refresh his email.

It came.

Jack did a half turn away from his bar mate and read…

"Jack, this is bad. I don't know what to do, but we need to do something and soon. Here are the links. Let me know what you're thinking. Miss you. MB."

Jack placed a trembling finger on the first link that exploded with a headline from the Lexington *Herald-Leader*:

FBI Probe Expands to Frankfort Lobbyists

"Oh, shit"

The second link took him to the Louisville *Courier Journal*.

Sources Say Arrests Likely in FBI Sting

"Oh, fuck"

The third from Pure Politics quoted unnamed sources giving up the names of lobbying firms being investigated by the feds for allegedly initiating a vote buying scheme that made BOPTROT look like kids ripping off CDs at Walmart.

There was a fourth link, a fifth, a sixth. Jack didn't need to read them. He couldn't turn his eyes away from the Pure Politics story that outed the firms under investigation. From his perspective, one name was far more prominent than the others — Barrows and Adams Strategic Solutions.

The words screamed at him! How did this happen? How did everything get so far out of hand?

At that moment, the phone rang. Mary Beth.

"Jack, what are we going to do?"

"Get in touch with Tony ASAP. Make sure you're on a secure line. Find out what the hell is going on and where we stand in this nightmare. I'm getting on a plane in five minutes. Pick me up at Blue Grass in about an hour. We need to meet. In person. All three of us. Tell Tony there are no ifs, ands or buts. We meet at his place in Frankfort 20 minutes after I land."

"Got it, Jack. I'm scared. So scared."

"Tony can fix this. That's what he does. Don't fret sweetie. Don't fret. Tony can fix this."

Jack's words were meant to calm and console Mary Beth. He didn't believe them. This is something even Tony couldn't fix, or if he could, he would need more luck than a Powerball winner.

"I'll see you in an hour, MB."

"I'll be waiting for you, Jack."

As the door shut and the plane started pushing back, Jack got a text from Mary Beth.

"Tony says the sun will come out tomorrow."

Jack was used to Tony speaking in code. It seems like that's all the three of them had done for months. This was a good sign. Tony apparently had found a way to fix their mounting problems. At least that's what he hoped the message meant. Were the situation more dire, the message would have been darker and foreboding — though still in code. Jack was convinced Tony had a book of quotes he trotted out to communicate with MB and him.

No matter. He breathed an uneasy sigh and punched a response into the phone.

"Message received. See you in an hour."

Jack put the phone in airplane mode and closed his eyes. He wouldn't sleep, couldn't if he wanted to. But the darkness gave him a little peace. He opened them long enough to fumble through his briefcase to find ear buds. He wasn't really listening to music, but no one else knew that and conversation with a stranger was the furthest thing from this mind. With his eyes shut and the engines lulling him, Jack relaxed more than he had in months. Still, his mind raced over what had happened and, more importantly, what could happen. How did a skinny kid from Belfry, Kentucky become the poster boy for political corruption in arguably the most corrupt state in the country?

The past is the past, Jack told himself. It can't be undone. But Tony would get them out of this mess. Tony was the fixer and nothing had ever needed fixing more than Barrows and Adams Strategic Solutions.

The minutes passed slowly. Jack checked his watch. It was the same time as it was when Mary Beth had called. The battery was dead. Time stood still — if only!

The captain squawked something unintelligible over the intercom. Below him, Jack could see the familiar trademark fences of Calumet Farm. The plane would touch down any minute. He knew Mary Beth would be waiting for him. Twenty minutes after setting foot on Kentucky soil, he'll sit with Tony in his Frankfort office.

Did he have a solution? Can the fixer still work his magic? In 20 minutes, MB and Jack would know.

Jack and Mary Beth arrived at 1 PP in record time. Tony motioned Jack into his great room with Mary Beth close behind. Shaughnessy was there. So was Flannery. There also were a couple of gubernatorial minions whose names escaped Jack. They had been part of the scheme to advance the Governor's legislative agenda. Now, they would be part of the solution to the shit storm brewing in the capitol, or at least that is what Jack was hoping.

On the island separating the great room and kitchen was a bottle of Maker's—half empty. Jack suspected that Tony and the others had a head start on him. He and MB would catch up quickly. Life's problems seem much more manageable with some 90-proof bourbon coursing through your veins.

"Were you followed," Tony asked.

"Of course I was followed," came the curt response. "What do you think this is? Law and Order? The bad guys elude the good guys? Christ, Tony, get in our reality. We have the full weight of the Justice Department, the FBI, the KBI and the Attorney General's office crashing down on us! It's not your job to worry about whether 'we're being followed,' but to fix the damn problem. That's what you do, right? Then fix the damn problem NOW."

The room fell quiet—deathly quiet. One of the minions reached into the ice bucket to freshen his drink and was greeted with looks that could kill from everyone else.

Mary Beth broke the uncomfortable silence, "It's almost 6:00. We need to turn on the news."

Tony had a wall of televisions in his house—eight in all so that he could watch multiple football and basketball games during betting season. But the programming now had nothing to do with covering a point spread.

WHAS was the first to report an FBI investigation that could reach all the way into the Governor's office and to the Speaker of the House.

WKYT was next. Then WLEX, WDRB, WLKY and on and on until every television outlet in Louisville and Lexington reported the news—all attributed to a special investigative report by the Frankfort *State Journal* and a reporter named Stuart Carroll.

Shaughnessy was not just a political whore, he was a media whore who subscribed to every news service known to mankind—real or fake. Between commercials for a car dealer and fast food restaurant, he got a text message from CNN.

"Whistle blower threatens to take down Kentucky government leaders."

A flick of the remotes and all eight televisions were dialed in to CNN doing a live interview from Frankfort with Stuart Carroll.

"To recap," said the news reader, "sources confirm that a Justice Department investigation is underway in Kentucky. Targets for the investigation reportedly involve Governor Damien Lyons, several members of his staff and legislative leadership including the Speaker of the House. More after this…"

How could there be more?

Minutes passed ever so slowly. Jack looked down at his watch again. Damn. Same time it was when he left Atlanta. The battery hadn't healed itself.

Not for Flannery. His phone started pinging with all manner of alerts from Kentucky news outlets. Tony took his cue from the phones.

"It's almost 8:00. Turn the TVs back on."

As minions one and two struggled with the elaborate remote system, Mary Beth lost all patience, stripped the device out of their hands and lit up the eight screens in front of them. A few minutes remained before the scheduled news conference, but all of the stations were running crawls—you know, the words crossing the bottom of the screen for special announcements, like an approaching storm. This was to be a storm unlike any other.

It looked almost like a Hollywood opening as lights scanned across the concrete façade of the John C. Watts Courthouse in Frankfort. While the collected crowd buzzed in anticipation, Tony and company cracked open their third bottle of Maker's and started passing it around. Leslye Pratt from WLEX was the first to break the television silence. MB switched all of the TVs to 18 News. Tony toasted the news reader — an alumnus of 1 PP — and thought to himself, at least she'll be fair, a delusion that lasted only a few seconds.

"Tom, Myra, in just moments, the U.S. Attorneys from Kentucky's Eastern and Western Districts will stand at this podium..." dramatic turn of the head and shoulder "...for an unusual joint press conference regarding federal grand jury investigations in Louisville, Lexington and here in Frankfort. We are told that the grand juries have been meeting since last November exploring allegations of government corruption and tonight, have handed up sealed indictments. Because they are sealed, we don't know how many have been accused, who they are or the nature of the allegations."

The camera zooned past her blonde hair to the podium where four people gathered.

"What the hell is she doing there?" Tony screamed as he had never screamed before.

'She' was Tamara Looney, Lieutenant Governor, liar, Judas, and working under cover for the FBI's latest sting.

Tony hurled his double old-fashion at the screens setting off an explosion of glass and bourbon as one TV fizzled to black. The other seven were still lit and staring with unblinking eyes at Tony, Jack, Mary Beth and the island of misfit boys at 1 PP.

"I'm Attorney General Robert Breckinridge and I have the unfortunate task of laying out the basics of a long and in-depth investigation by the FBI, the KBI in my office, and various other law enforcement agencies. Together, we have unearthed a trail of alleged government corruption that leads all the way to the Capitol."

Anyone knowledgeable of the capitol floor plan knows the only office holders who call the dome home are, the AG and Lt. Governor, both of whom were at the press conference, Clarence Nolan, the doddering Secretary of State whose only brush with corruption came in the 1980s when someone gave him a free plane ride to an out-of-state conference, and, the *big one*, Governor Damien Lyons. How was he involved? What was the nature of the corruption? Why could reporters not find him or Flannery? How long had he been involved in whatever this nightmare was? Allegedly.

AG Breckinridge continued.

"Joining me tonight are Stan Duncan and Karen Wilson, U.S. Attorneys from Eastern and Western Districts of Kentucky who helped guide the investigation, which has resulted in 47 sealed indictments being handed up tonight by the three grand juries impaneled in Louisville, Lexington and Frankfort.

"Also joining us is Lt. Governor Tamara Looney whose office played a pivotal role in exposing the breadth and depth of the corruption being alleged."

Tony fired a second bourbon bomb at an unfortunate wide screen,

"Damn her. Damn her soul to hell!"

Minions one and two looked at each other in disbelief. They had unwittingly helped set the snare that would trap themselves and dozens of others. Minion two started crying.

Shaughnessy joined Tony in his own curse-fest. Flannery plopped down in an overstuffed leather chair with three fingers of bourbon and said nothing.

Bridget wasn't around for the nightmare that was about to worsen significantly. She had run to Louisville on an errand. Truth be told, though, she was in Shelbyville with Agent Whitney, her troops, and her reinforcements.

March 20 was an historic day in Kentucky for politicians, political kingmakers, business owners, and the media. Stuart Carroll was riding a killer wave of adrenaline. He was the darling of political media across the country for the story he broke in little, old Frankfort.

March 21 would be even more historic.

Chapter 46 — A date that will live in infamy

March 21 is an auspicious date. It was on that day that the first rock-and-roll concert was staged in Cleveland back in 1952; in 1970, the first Earth Day was proclaimed (California, of course); President Jimmy Carter announced a boycott of the 1980 Summer Olympics in Moscow; and Twitter was launched in 2006.

March 21 was also the day when Frankfort came completely unglued.

Darren Peavler's obituary occupied about four column-inches in the *State Journal*. Page 8, below the fold, which was dominated by a continuation of the front-page story about the federal investigation.

SB 44 was dead. Pulled from the Orders of the Day, which were delayed because of the myriad eulogies on the floor of the House for its sponsor. Not to be outdone, the Senate dedicated the remainder of the session to Peavler and delayed the Orders of the Day to allow members to offer their own perspectives on the leadership, integrity, and compassion that he had demonstrated throughout his life.

HB 417, though, was very much alive, despite the adverse publicity and threats of an indictment that loomed before supporters. Not for long.

As the Clerk was about to call HB 417 for a vote, FBI agents, state police, and investigators from the KBI stormed into the Senate chambers and started picking off legislators who had been named in the indictments, which had now been unsealed.

Down the hall, another contingent of law enforcement officials descended on the House even as Speaker Patrick was offering his condolences to the Peavler family. Patrick was handcuffed and taken into custody. Many of his supporters, including chairman Kerr, were dragged off the floor as well.

The early reports were wrong. The investigation was farther reaching than the media had speculated based on Stuart's report. The specific charges varied depending on the person involved, but let the record show that indictments were returned against:

- Governor Damien Lyons
- Chief of Staff Jimmy Flannery
- House Speaker Teddy Patrick
- Senate President Larry Offutt
- Various members of the House and Senate, including Chairman Kerr, who compromised their positions by agreeing to vote as leadership directed with a cash payment waiting in the wings
- Riley Shaughnessy
- Clement Combs
  And then the "innocent" bystanders started to fall.
- Mary Beth Corrigan
- Amber
- Melanie
- Melissa
- A host of other Hooters' wannabes
- The Bosnian cleaning ladies
- Even Hannah in Naples

The biggest guns of them all were also in their crosshairs, Jack Adams and Tony Barrows. The feds, and local FPD, had them on a number of charges from influence peddling to promoting prostitution.

The raids on the House and Senate were unnerving. More unnerving, though, was the fact that so much more information on different levels of corruption could and would now be exposed in both chambers when the case made it to court.

Chapter 47 — All the King's Men

In 1947, Robert Penn Warren won a Pulitzer Prize for his novel, *All the King's Men*. It chronicled the rise and fall of a Southern politician named Willie Stark. And as the name implies from the Humpty Dumpty nursery rhyme, All the King's Horses and All the King's Men Couldn't Put Humpty Together Again.

Spoiler alert in case you have never read the novel, Willie Stark dies at the end — shot to death in the capitol. No one died when the raids started in Kentucky. Of course, Darren Peavler went down the day before all hell broke loose, and Dave Tunie ended his own life when the dominoes started to fall in Frankfort.

For some, though, death may have been a welcome alternative to the hell they and their families would face in the weeks and months to come. Subpoenas begat separations. Separations begat divorces. Custody battles ensued. Finger-pointing became the new audience participation sport. Had there been a revolving door on the federal courthouse, it likely would have been worn into submission.

The only winners? The attorneys — the high-profile suits from Lexington, Louisville, Nashville, D.C., and elsewhere. The locals who were lost balls in high weeds. They may have been licensed to practice at the federal level but were woefully ill-equipped to do so.

After the initial round of arraignments, which included a well-choreographed perp walk for the former movers and shakers, the deals started coming so fast that a used car salesman would be hard-pressed to keep up.

TV police dramas have made the phrase so commonplace that we assume it to be true: Whoever talks first gets the best deal.

And there were plenty of bait fish who wanted to talk about the trophies the FBI and Justice Department were really after. Of course, there were still consequences to pay. The innocent bystanders, like the M&M girls, Hannah, and some of the other babes in the bunch faced financial ruin because being one of Tony's playthings didn't pay enough to afford the attorneys they had to retain. None of the elected officials who were indicted would ever seek office again.

Their days as public servants—a title which is laughable in these circumstances—were over. The civilians, like Riley Shaughnessy and Jimmy Flannery, would take a fall just as Humpty Dumpty did, but it wasn't so great that they couldn't overcome the humiliation of a few years in federal prison. Minions one and two would follow a similar path.

The trophies were yet to be landed: Clement Combs, Jack Adams, Damien Lyons, Tony Barrows, and Mary Beth Corrigan. Yes, Mary Beth Corrigan. Because of her relationship with Tony and Jack, and her knowledge of what was transpiring on HB 417, the feds wanted her just as badly as they did Tony and Jack.

With Bridget as the source for much of what had happened over the past six months, Mary Beth was surely toast. Bridget cried in MB's arms when the arrest was first made. She cried every time she visited Mary Beth in lockup. For her part, Mary Beth was forgiving. She showed no ill will toward Bridget, who was only doing what the feds had forced her to do. MB had played along with Tony's game. She is the one who used her guile, sex appeal, and artistic abilities to feed Tony's insatiable quest for power. She had reached the top rung of Frankfort's social and power ladder along with Tony and Jack. She would now have to pay the price. The meteoric rise was about to give way to a meteoric crash. Until…

Chapter 48 – Oh, what a tangled web

No one fell as hard and fast as Damien Lyons. Sitting governors rarely go down in flames, and when they do, it reverberates throughout the political universe. Lyons initially challenged the allegations and vowed to fight to maintain his position as governor – and as a Senate candidate against Micha McDougal. That bluster and bravado didn't last long. As the evidence started to mount and rats like Jimmy Flannery started to abandon ship, Lyons was, himself, in the awkward position of trying to negotiate his own settlement. That became abundantly more difficult when his old friend, Aaron Miller from Georgia, turned on his McCallie School buddy rather than face his own indictment for some questionable campaign contributions funneled Lyons' way.

Once he announced his resignation from office "to devote all of my time to defending my good name and that of my family," Tamara Looney became governor – the first woman to hold the office since Martha Layne Collins won an election in 1983. Looney strapped on her law and order gun belt, brought on the AG Breckinridge as her Lieutenant, and became a media darling, not only in Kentucky but also at a national level. There was even premature mention of a slot on the next Democratic presidential campaign as Veep regardless of who topped the ticket.

In addition to Breckinridge, Governor Looney surrounded herself with appointees who had been involved with the investigation, or who had kept their noses clean while the legislative shenanigans played out. One of the more interesting appointments was that of Stuart Carroll to be her Chief Communications Officer – a glorified title for press secretary.

Stuart was being rewarded with a significant pay increase, a seat at the governor's leadership table, and to top it all, a Pulitzer of his own for investigative reporting.

Rachel Whitney declined the governor's invitation to become Lieutenant Governor. But she did succumb to the siren's call of Washington and a special agent in charge designation for the entire southeastern section of the country.

Roscoe Bodine was a killing machine. He had proven it to his boss, Clement, time and time again. Before that, he had proven it to another boss, Uncle Sam. But Roscoe wasn't the sharpest knife in the drawer. He had slipped into Darren Peavler's apartment and put a .22 slug in his head as he had done too many times before to other victims. The problem was, neither he nor Clement suspected that video cameras had been installed outside on State Street, and in every room of the apartment. The feds were close by when Roscoe pulled the trigger, but not close enough to stop him. When Roscoe was arrested by State Police on murder charges, he started singing louder than any coal mine canary.

Clement made me do this. Clement hired me to do that. Everything bad I have done since I left the service was because of Clement.

Roscoe pulled no punches. He was going down for 25 to life, but he dodged the death penalty.

Clement would not be so lucky. The only point of contention was who would get first crack at him—the state or the feds. In either case, he was going away for life without parole. At his advanced age, that may not be too long, and it would be without Hannah or any other conquests the philanderer from Phelps had enjoyed—much more cruel than the sentence itself.

Jack ran. It did no good, but he ran nonetheless. He hopped a jet that Clement kept parked at the Frankfort airport and headed to a small island off the coast of Belize—an island Clement owned. Jack thought he could avoid extradition there. He was wrong.

When he was returned to the states, he faced the full furor of prosecutors and the judge who had allowed him to be free while awaiting trial. He was in cuffs when U.S. Marshal's brought him onto Kentucky soil at the Louisville airport. His trial would be delayed for several months because of motions, hearings, appeals, etc. He, however, remained behind bars for the entire time. His days as a flight risk were over.

Then, there was Tony. The biggest fish in the pond. He had people lining up to take him down. The girls, the legislators, Flannery and Shaughnessy, crooked cops, wire upon wire, and of course, Bridget. But like Mary Beth, Tony was forgiving of Bridget and the unenviable job she was forced to fulfill for the feds.

He knew he was done, and took it all in stride. He sent flowers and a note of congratulations to Tamara Looney after she was sworn in as governor. Agent Whitney also received a bouquet and a simple note that said, "Checkmate. You win. Good job, Agent Whitney."

This was not the southside of Frankfort. This was the bigtime, and the big players all lined up for a piece of Tony — the media, the attorneys, the writers, and even a film producer who said he and Ridley Scott were close. Of course, his credibility was very much in doubt when he called his friend of Riley Scott.

Still, Big Tony was a poster boy for all things wrong with politics in the U.S. He just happened to get caught. It's not illegal if you don't get caught. That is how he was brought up, or at least that's what he told himself. But this was not Mrs. Walker's cat. He had been caught; he had been tried in the press; he had been found guilty in the court of public opinion. There was only one thing to do. He offered his own plea agreement. He would plead no contest to all charges against him. In exchange, he would offer testimony against his co-conspirators, alive and dead. The only thing he asked in exchange was that any and all charges against Mary Beth be dropped. He painted her as a victim, drawn into the world of power and politics by people with unscrupulous motives — people like himself. If the feds would give Mary Beth a "get out of jail free card," he would do whatever necessary to bring others to justice.

Prosecutors thought they had hit the lottery. Tony's testimony would supersede other deals that had been struck because he was able to offer testimony on crimes that had been committed before the FBI investigation was launched — crimes that would add years to those already in the system and that would bring in a host of new players that had been involved in previous Frankfort felonies. The who's who of Kentucky politics was about to gain some new chapters in the section on corruption.

All the feds had to give up was Mary Beth — small price to pay to land Tony without a struggle, plus the cadre of cads he was bringing with him. The spousal immunity he had hinted at when they married was never invoked. He brought himself down, and in the process, saved her.

Bridget was there to meet Mary Beth when she was released from the Frankfort jail cell that had been her home for five weeks. They fell into each other's arms and both wept. Tears of joy at being free for Mary Beth; tears of remorse from Bridget that she had betrayed her friend and lover.

As they made their way to Bridget's car, someone Mary Beth worked with at LRC caught them on the street.

"Did you hear? Did you hear what happened to Tony?"

Neither had heard anything. The friend walked hastily away as if late for an appointment. They had no clue about what was going on or what the questions had meant. It wasn't long after they reached Bridget's car that the radio news let them know what had happened.

Chapter 49—The bigger they are

Tony's deal had one other condition beyond Mary Beth's clemency: he had to have full access to the amenities at 1PP while awaiting sentencing. That meant his multi-screen TV set up to catch MLB games; it meant the home theatre to watch a hastily purchased porn collection—after all, where he was going, sex with anything in a skirt was going to be a fleeting memory; it meant trading shots of new single-barrel bourbons with Marshals who were happy to look the other way, except when the porn was running and then it was all eyes front; and it meant playing golf on his three-hole course, without the lovely cup caddies on Number Two.

With the exception of so many crew cuts with badges, it was essentially business as usual at 1PP, although the Bosnian cleaning ladies were sorely missed.

It was the Monday after Derby—the first Run for the Roses Tony had missed in 10 years. He told the deputy in charge that he wanted to play a round or two before lunch. He invited the deputy to join him. There were extra clubs in the garage—probably some shoes to fit as well.

The two climbed aboard the John Deere Gator—Tony's personal redneck golf cart that had been fitted with new shoes so as not to tear up the fairways. They played the personal course three times before coming back to the house for beverages and a bite of lunch. Tony had shot an opening 42; Deputy Stanton was at 44. Tony whipped up a club sandwich and offered the other deputies on duty their own, which they happily accepted. The midday meal would have been so much better had the Bosnian's been there. The Marshals agreed with Tony's assessment.

While the Marshals munched on their sandwiches, Tony returned to the Gator. He reached his hand under the seat to retrieve a fifth of Makers for the back nine. But the big bear paw that was one of his signatures became stuck between the seat and the floor.

"Hey, Stanton," he said nonplussed. "A little help here."

The deputies could see that Tony was in a bit of a jam and hastened to help their host as best they could.

"Here, let me grab your wrist," said Stanton.

"OWW. Damn, John, you trying to cut off my hand?"

"Someone go inside and get some soap. We'll lather up the hand and slide it out."

Two deputies scurried from the deck—one to the kitchen and one to the bath, both looking for a lubricant to grease the wrist.

Three others remained in limbo between the deck and the Gator. Only Stanton was near Tony. When he backed away from the vehicle, Tony shouted.

"Oh my God. The throttle is stuck. The throttle is stuck!"

With that, the green Gator went screaming toward the cliff. Tony's hand was still firmly locked beneath the seat. Deputy Stanton and others went racing toward the accelerating cart. It would likely be stopped by the barriers that were in place to prevent drunks from plummeting to their death. But as the deputies lost more and more ground to the Gator, they saw that the cables were missing. Tony moved faster away from the deputies who were in hot pursuit. The cables were not there to stop him. He crashed through a wild sumac tree growing on the cliff's edge and went sailing downward toward the river and rapids below him.

The deputies stopped abruptly in total disbelief. There was nothing to do except watch Big Tony plummet to his death some 10 stories down the palisade cliffs into the murky waters that sliced through Kentucky.

It takes fewer than 3 seconds for a mass like the Gator and Tony to fall more than 100 feet. But that was plenty of time for Tony to raise both hands skyward toward the deputies and flip them off. Yes, both hands. Yes, two fingers. Yes, flipping off the authorities.

The calls went out immediately to 9-1-1, to EMTs and the local water rescue guys. Their search was for naught. Tony wasn't found; the Gator was. When it was extracted from the water, there was no sign of blood, skin, or anything else that would point to Tony being stuck. There also was no evidence of a Maker's bottle beneath the seat.

Had they seen right? Did Tony actually flip them off with both hands, including the one that was inextricably stuck?

The coroner, absent a body, ruled death by accident. The eyewitnesses, U.S. Marshals, conveyed what they saw, and who could argue with that credibility. Tony was dead. There was no body, but the evidence was overwhelming. The big guy from South Frankfort was no more; nor were the schemes he relished in developing. Of course, the big guy from South Frankfort had one last scheme.

The coroner had been paid a nice stipend in cash to rule the death an accident. He knew it wasn't; Tony knew it wasn't going to be. But the insurance company needed assurance that the death was not suicide in order to pay the beneficiary — double indemnity since it was an accident, not the old *film noir*, rather a real case of spoils to the victor. But who?

In Frankfort, there are three kinds of lawyers: those who work for the government; those who work to make a decent living; and those whose sole work is to attend to the rich and powerful. Enter Scott Bare.

Bare was the attorney Tony hired in advance of his death to deal with his estate. The agreement was struck long before the FBI investigation, became a matter of public discourse.

Following Tony's accident, Bare called three people to his office. The first was Bridget O'Shea, although neither could really figure out why. The second was Mary Beth Corrigan, who was — at least in name — Tony's wife. The third was Father Tim O'Shea — which caught everyone in attendance by complete surprise since the two had never met.

Bare started his dissertation in the same baritone voice he used in his church choir.

"I, Anthony DeMarco Barrows, being of sound mind and body…"

The litany could be spelled out in its entirety, but unlike lawyers, you are not being paid by the hour. In a nutshell:

- 1PP and its furnishings were to be auctioned to the highest bidder with all proceeds going to Father Timothy for use in his ministry with disadvantaged youth in Louisville's west end.
- The condo in Orange Beach and a nearby commercial building were bequeathed to Bridget O'Shea for her personal enjoyment and professional use. This was the condo where the three had stayed. Bridget thought it was a rental. Tony had owned it for years and saw how much Bridget had enjoyed it. The office building across the street was simply a bonus.
- "and to my lovely wife, Mary Beth…" The marriage of convenience that the two had embarked on so many months ago was now about to bear fruit for Mary Beth — tremendous fruit — though she really wanted none of it.

Bottom line, the remainder of Tony's estate, including a $4 million life insurance policy, was hers. She was overcome with disbelief and collapsed at the feet of Scott Bare, esquire. Both Tim and Bridget rushed to console — and revive — her.

Chapter 50 — Calling the Redneck Rivera Home

Tony's death had been a blow to those who loved him, including those who saw nothing but prison bars in their future, like Jack Adams. For those on the outside, it was even tougher. But they managed to step up and try to make Tony proud, or at least appreciative of what they were about to do.

Tim, or Father Timothy, did exactly as Tony had commanded. Using the proceeds of the 1PP auction — some $1.75 million — he opened a community center at the corner of 42nd and Broadway that focused entirely on early childhood education and school readiness.

Bridget made the condo her own; her own taste in decorating; a total remodel of the kitchen; the addition of a spa tub in the master bedroom — with a wall knocked out to overlook the Gulf at sunset. Her desire for the good things seemed to have no end.

One of those good things was Mary Beth. All was forgiven, as if there were any doubt. They lived together in the condo. Mary Beth took space in the building across the street to showcase her artistic talent. "Sugar and Spice." That was the name of the gallery. On the left side was sugar, with the Norman Rockwell poses for families on vacation or snowbirds looking for the perfect Christmas gift. On the right was spice, which involved sexier paintings of newlywed wives wanting the keep the honeymoon alive, those of the more senior variety who wanted a little spark, just as Chairman Kerr did with Amber, or the housewife who thought the hubby was taking her for granted,

The constant was Tony. In the lobby, a life-size portrait adorned the office with Mary Beth and Bridget painted in the best possible cross between Rockwell and Vargas as MB could muster. They stood in sexual splendor; between them, seated in a leather wing chair, was Tony. The small brass plaque on the frame that surrounded them was inscribed with a simple "Our Chairman."

The tan, but freckled Irish lass on one side. The pale, raven-haired beauty on the other. And the larger than life figure that was Tony Barrows seated between them — forever in this pose. On his wrist, a replica of the Rolex that had both beguiled his casual acquaintances and betrayed him with those outside his circle. It would forever more be fixed at 5:00.

Epilogue

Sugar and Spice was wildly successful — more than Mary Beth or Bridget could ever have imagined. Tourists and townies came from as far away as Destin and Panama City in the east to Biloxi and New Orleans in the west. All wanted a sitting with Mary Beth. She was a regional sensation featured on TV news, in lifestyle publications, and the travel section of newspapers, magazines, and online travel guides.

For her part, Bridget managed the books and the home fires. All was good. Both were as happy and content as they had ever been in their lives.

One day, in late September when the warm breeze off the Gulf was taking on a bit of chill, Bridget came crashing through the door to the Spice section of the studio. Mary Beth was working with an ER nurse who was wearing a stethoscope and little else — an early Christmas present for the ER doc who worked her shift.

MB was not happy. She hated interruptions — even from Bridget. But there was no other way to reach her since there was no response to calls or texts.

"He's alive, Mary Beth. Tony is alive!"

Mary Beth handed the bewildered model a robe and asked her to have a seat in the lounge for a bit.

Once the nurse had left the room, Mary Beth responded — rather strongly, "Impossible! That can't be true! He fell from a 100-foot cliff."

"I know that. You know that. The U.S. Marshals know that. But I swear to God that I saw him in Publix—full beard, different color hair, but I know it was him."

"I still say it's impossible. We all have a 'twin' somewhere. This has to be Tony's. He can't be alive."

"I'm telling you, it was Tony. He even had the same laugh when he cracked a joke with the butcher."

"It can't be true, but even if it is, why here and why now? You don't just return from the dead after 18 months."

Bridget started to respond—to try and rationalize what she had seen, or at least what she thought she saw. Her words, already sputtering, were abruptly interrupted by a, "Hello," spoken loud enough from the lobby that it easily could be heard in the Spice rack.

In the foyer was a teenager—a poster boy for acne cream, but it was the package that he carried that grabbed their attention. Cradled in his hands was a small, foam cooler with a bright red bow as big as the cooler itself.

Mary Beth took the package, still quite bewildered. Bridget fumbled for some cash to tip the teen.

"Not necessary, ma'am. It has already been taken care of."

"By whom," Bridget inquired anxiously.

"Didn't catch his name, but he could be that guy's brother," at which point he motioned toward the painting looming over them.

Mary Beth and Bridget exchanged wary stares. MB removed the bow and the lid. Inside was a bottle of Bulleit bourbon and the largest sea scallops either had ever seen. There was also a note.

Bourbon-glazed scallops are the best seafood you will ever put in your mouth if you know exactly how to <u>FIX</u> them. Love you both, Big T.

26008009R00163

Made in the USA
Lexington, KY
20 December 2018